ALSO BY MICHAEL CUNNINGHAM

A
WILD SWAN

A WILD SWAN

AND OTHER TALES

MICHAEL CUNNINGHAM

ILLUSTRATED BY YUKO SHIMIZU

FARRAR, STRAUS AND GIROUX

NEW YORK

Farrar, Straus and Giroux
18 West 18th Street, New York 10011

Printed in the United States of America
First edition, 2015

The following stories originally appeared, in slightly different
form, in *Document*: "Crazy Old Lady" (as "Hansel and Gretel"),
"A Monkey's Paw," and "A Wild Swan."

Library of Congress Cataloging-in-Publication Data
Cunningham, Michael, 1952–
    [Short stories. Selections]
    A wild swan : and other tales / Michael Cunningham ; illustrated by
Yuko Shimizu.
        pages ; cm
    ISBN 978-0-374-29025-2 (hardcover) — ISBN 978-0-374-71260-0
(ebook)
    I. Shimizu, Yuko, 1965– illustrator.   II. Title.

PS3553.U484 A6 2015
813'.54—dc23

                                                        2015002963

Designed by Jonathan D. Lippincott

Our books may be purchased in bulk for promotional, educational, or
business use. Please contact your local bookseller or the Macmillan Corporate
and Premium Sales Department at 1-800-221-7945, extension 5442,
or by e-mail at MacmillanSpecialMarkets@macmillan.com.

www.fsgbooks.com
www.twitter.com/fsgbooks • www.facebook.com/fsgbooks

1   3   5   7   9   10   8   6   4   2

CONTENTS

A
WILD SWAN

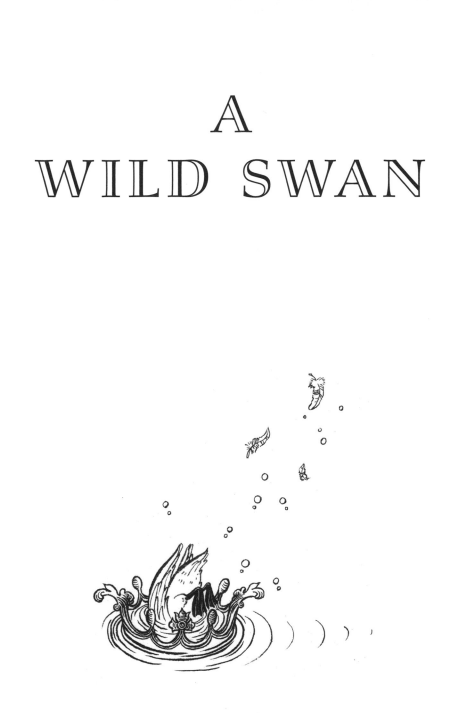

DIS. ENCHANT.

Most of us are safe. If you're not a delirious dream the gods are having, if your beauty doesn't trouble the constellations, nobody's going to cast a spell on you. No one wants to transform you into a beast, or put you to sleep for a hundred years. The wraith disguised as a pixie isn't thinking of offering you three wishes, with doom hidden in them like a razor in a cake.

The middling maidens—the ones best seen by candlelight, corseted and rouged—have nothing to worry about. The pudgy, pockmarked heirs apparent, who torment their underlings and need to win at every game, are immune to curse and hex. B-list virgins do not excite the forces of ruination; callow swains don't infuriate demons and sprites.

Most of us can be counted on to manage our own undoings. Vengeful entities seek only to devastate the rarest, the ones who have somehow been granted not only bower and trumpet but comeliness that startles the birds in the trees, coupled with grace, generosity, and charm so effortless as to seem like ordinary human qualities.

Who wouldn't want to fuck these people up? Which of us

does not understand, in our own less presentable depths, the demons and wizards compelled to persecute human mutations clearly meant, by deities thinking only of their own entertainment, to make almost everyone feel even lonelier and homelier, more awkward, more doubtful and blamed, than we actually are?

If certain manifestations of perfection can be disgraced, or disfigured, or sent to walk the earth in iron shoes, the rest of us will find ourselves living in a less arduous world; a world of more reasonable expectations; a world in which the appellations "beauty" and "potency" can be conferred upon a larger cohort of women and men. A world where praise won't be accompanied by an implied willingness to overlook a few not-quite qualities, a little bit of less-than.

Please ask yourself. If you could cast a spell on the ludicrously handsome athlete and the lingerie model he loves, or on the wedded movie stars whose combined DNA is likely to produce children of another species entirely . . . would you? Does their aura of happiness and prosperity, their infinite promise, irritate you, even a little? Does it occasionally make you angry?

If not, blessings on you.

If so, however, there are incantations and ancient songs, there are words to be spoken at midnight, during certain phases of the moon, beside bottomless lakes hidden deep in the woods, or in secret underground chambers, or at any point where three roads meet.

These curses are surprisingly easy to learn.

A WILD SWAN

ere in the city lives a prince whose left arm is like any other man's and whose right arm is a swan's wing.

He and his eleven brothers were turned into swans by their vituperative stepmother, who had no intention of raising the twelve sons of her husband's former wife (whose pallid, mortified face stared glassily from portrait after portrait; whose unending pregnancies had dispatched her before her fortieth birthday). Twelve brawling, boastful boys; twelve fragile and rapacious egos; twelve adolescences—all presented to the new queen as routine aspects of her job. Do we blame her? Do we, really?

She turned the boys into swans, and commanded them to fly away.

Problem solved.

She spared the thirteenth child, the youngest, because she was a girl, though the stepmother's fantasies about shared confidences and daylong shopping trips evaporated quickly enough. Why, after all, would a girl be anything but surly and petulant toward the woman who'd turned her brothers into birds? And so—after a certain patient lenience toward sulking silences, after a number of ball gowns purchased but never worn—the queen gave up. The princess lived in the castle like an impoverished relative, fed and housed, tolerated but not loved.

The twelve swan-princes lived on a rock far out at sea, and were permitted only an annual, daylong return to their kingdom, a visit that was both eagerly anticipated and awkward for the king and his consort. It was hard to exult in a day spent among twelve formerly stalwart and valiant sons who could only, during that single yearly interlude, honk and preen and peck at mites as they flapped around in the castle courtyard. The king did his best at pretending to be glad to see them. The queen was always struck by one of her migraines.

Years passed. And then . . . At long last . . .

On one of the swan-princes' yearly furloughs, their little sister broke the spell, having learned from a beggar woman she met while picking berries in the forest that the only known cure for the swan transformation curse was coats made of nettles.

However. The girl was compelled to knit the coats in secret, because they needed (or so the beggar woman told her) not only to be made of nettles, but of nettles collected from graveyards, after dark. If the princess was caught gathering nettles from among tombstones, past midnight, her stepmother would surely have accused her of witchcraft, and had her burned along with the rest of the garbage. The girl, no fool, knew she couldn't count on her father, who by then harbored a

secret wish (which he acknowledged not even to himself) to be free of all his children.

The princess crept nightly into local graveyards to gather nettles, and spent her days weaving them into coats. It was, as it turned out, a blessing that no one in the castle paid much attention to her.

She had almost finished the twelve coats when the local archbishop (who was not asked why he himself happened to be in a graveyard so late at night) saw her picking nettles, and turned her in. The queen felt confirmed in her suspicions (this being the girl who shared not a single virginal secret, who claimed complete indifference to shoes exquisite enough to be shown in museums). The king, unsurprisingly, acceded, hoping he'd be seen as strong and unsentimental, a true king, a king so devoted to protecting his people from the darker forces that he'd agree to the execution of his own daughter, if it kept his subjects safe, free of curses, unafraid of demonic transformations.

Just as the princess was about to be tied to the stake, however, the swan-brothers descended from the smoky sky, and their sister threw the coats onto them. Suddenly, with a loud crackling sound, amid a flurry of sparkling wind, twelve studly young men, naked under their nettle coats, stood in the courtyard, with only a few stray white feathers wafting around them.

Actually . . .

. . . there were eleven fully intact princes and one, the twelfth, restored save for a single detail—his right arm remained a swan's wing, because his sister, interrupted at her work, had had to leave one coat with a missing sleeve.

It seemed a small-enough price to pay.

Eleven of the young men soon married, had children, joined organizations, gave parties that thrilled everyone, right down to the mice in the walls. Their thwarted stepmother, so raucously outnumbered, so unmotherly, retreated to a convent, which inspired the king to fabricate memories of abiding loyalty to his transfigured sons and helplessness before his harridan of a wife, a version the boys were more than willing to believe.

End of story. "Happily ever after" fell on everyone like a guillotine's blade.

Almost everyone.

It was difficult for the twelfth brother, the swan-winged one. His father, his uncles and aunts, the various lords and ladies, were not pleased by the reminder of their brush with such sinister elements, or their unskeptical willingness to execute the princess as she worked to save her siblings.

The king's court made jokes about the swan-winged prince, which his eleven flawlessly formed brothers took up readily, insisting they were meant only in fun. The young nieces and nephews, children of the eleven brothers, hid whenever the twelfth son entered a room, and giggled from behind the chaises and tapestries. His brothers' wives asked repeatedly that he do his best to remain calm at dinner (he was prone to gesticulating with the wing while telling a joke, and had once flicked an entire haunch of venison against the opposite wall). The palace cats tended to snarl and slink away whenever he came near.

Finally he packed a few things and went out into the world. The world, however, proved no easier for him than the palace had been. He could get only the most menial of jobs. He had no marketable skills (princes don't), and just one working hand. Every now and then a woman grew interested, but it always turned out that she was briefly drawn to some Leda fantasy or, worse, hoped her love could bring him back his arm. Nothing ever lasted. The wing was awkward on the subway, impossible in cabs. It had to be checked constantly for lice. And unless it was washed daily, feather by feather, it turned from the creamy white of a French tulip to a linty, dispiriting gray.

He lived with his wing as another man might live with a dog adopted from the pound: sweet-tempered, but neurotic and untrainable. He loved his wing, helplessly. He also found it exasperating, adorable, irritating, wearying, heartbreaking. It embarrassed him, not only because he didn't manage to keep it cleaner, or because getting through doors and turnstiles never got less awkward, but because he failed to insist on it as an asset. Which wasn't all that hard to imagine. He could see himself selling himself as a compelling mutation, a young god, proud to the point of sexy arrogance of his anatomical deviation: ninety percent thriving muscled man-flesh and ten percent glorious blindingly white angel wing.

Baby, these feathers are going to tickle you halfway to heaven, and this man-part is going to take you the rest of the way.

Where, he asked himself, was that version of him? What dearth of nerve rendered him, as year followed year, increasingly paunchy and slack-shouldered, a walking apology? Why was it beyond his capacities to get back into shape, to cop an attitude, to stroll insouciantly into clubs in a black lizardskin suit with one sleeve cut off?

Yeah, right, sweetheart, it's a wing, I'm part angel, but trust me, the rest is pure devil.

He couldn't seem to manage that. He might as well have tried to run a three-minute mile, or become a virtuoso on the violin.

He's still around. He pays his rent one way or another. He takes his love where he can find it. In late middle age he's grown ironic, and cheerful in a toughened, seen-it-all way. He's become possessed of a world-weary wit. He's realized he can either descend into bitterness or become a wised-up holy fool. It's better, it's less mortifying, to be the guy who understands that the joke's on him, and is the first to laugh when the punch line lands.

Most of his brothers back at the palace are on their second or third wives. Their children, having been cosseted and catered to all their lives, can be difficult. The princes spend their days knocking golden balls into silver cups, or skewering moths with their swords. At night they watch the jesters and jugglers and acrobats perform.

The twelfth brother can be found, most nights, in one of the bars on the city's outer edges, the ones that cater to people who were only partly cured of their curses, or not cured at all. There's the three-hundred-year-old woman who wasn't specific enough when she spoke to the magic fish, and found herself crying, "No, wait, I meant alive and *young* forever," into a suddenly empty sea. There's the crownletted frog who can't seem to truly love any of the women willing to kiss him, and break the spell. There's the prince who's spent years trying to determine the location of the comatose princess he's meant to revive with a kiss, and has lately been less devoted to searching mountain and glen, more prone to bar-crawling, given to long stories about the girl who got away.

In such bars, a man with a single swan wing is considered lucky.

His life, he tells himself, is not the worst of all possible lives. Maybe that's enough. Maybe that's what there is to hope for— that it merely won't get any worse.

Some nights, when he's stumbled home smashed (there are many such nights), negotiated the five flights up to his apartment, turned on the TV, and passed out on the sofa, he awakes, hours later, as the first light grays the slats of the venetian blinds, with only his hangover for company, to find that he's curled his wing over his chest and belly; or rather (he knows this to be impossible, and yet . . .) that the wing has curled itself, by its own volition, over him, both blanket and companion, his devoted resident alien, every bit as imploring and ardent and inconvenient as that mutt from the pound would have been. His dreadful familiar. His burden, his comrade.

CRAZY OLD LADY

t's the solitude that slays you. Maybe because you'd expected ruin to arrive in a grander and more romantic form.

You ran, as your mother put it, with a fast crowd. You threw off your schoolgirl plaids early, lied your way to adulthood in taverns three towns away, encouraged the men there to put first their fingers and then other parts into whatever interlude of skin you were able to offer them in the dimness of alleys, the little patches of neglected grass that passed for parks.

You went through three husbands, and joked to your girl-friends that with each marriage you'd thought you'd reached bottom, only to find that the elevator of love went to still lower floors. You decided against husband number four because, by then, even you could see the nascent defeat in his plans for the future. You could hear the muttered, gin-marinated accusations to come.

After you'd dispatched the fourth candidate, you embarked on a career of harshly jovial sluttishness. You were in your forties. By then your girlfriends had all married tolerable men and gradually, over time, found more and more reasons not to meet you for drinks (*Sorry, but the children wear me out; I'd love to, but you know how my husband gets when I come home loaded*).

It struck you, during your forties and then your fifties, as a personal victory. You weren't sweeping splintery floorboards as your husband sat bemoaning the bleak fate you'd helped make for him, the job that barely paid for heat and light; you weren't pressing a fifth infant to breasts increasingly unwilling to produce more than thimblefuls of milk. Your solution to your slackening body was squeezing it into ever-tighter dresses until, by the time sixty loomed, it seemed as if the dresses themselves held you upright on the bar stools; that if they were cut away, you'd spill onto the floor and lie there, helpless, a pink-white muddle of overused flesh.

You let that lost tooth remain a black square in your knowing smile. You dyed your hair: circus orange, followed by a maroon deep enough to verge on purple, followed by white-hot blond.

You were undeluded. You believed you were undeluded. You were thinking, "House of the Rising Sun"—a wised-up, whorish finish, with its scattered rhinestones still sewn on here and there. You imagined, in the long run, a perversely glorious, housebound lasciviousness; a reputation for insanity among the zealots who worshipped banal virtues as if they were glory incarnate. You expected late-night visits from the local young bucks (yes, you thought about your old girlfriends' sons), in search of the instruction you'd provide (*Put your fingertip there, right there, pinch gently, very gently, I promise you she'll love it*); boys who'd be grateful for the nights of ecstatic transport you'd visit upon them, and, more touching still, for the mornings they'd wake with faces buried in your breasts, abashed, embarrassed, eager to depart, in which endeavor you'd encourage them (you'd cultivate no hint of desperation, never urge them to stay). During the brief interludes before they jumped up to search for their socks and underwear, you'd assure them that they were marvels, they were warriors; gifts in the making for some girl who'd be thankful forever for what you'd taught them in a single night.

The boys would grin with nervous self-admiration as they stumbled back into their clothes. They'd know the truth when they heard it. They'd understand: You were seeding your town with suitable husbands. You were a goddess (a minor goddess, but still) of carnal knowingness; you were seeing to it that the youth of the region knew not only where the clitoris is, but what to do with it. You were cultivating, in absentia, a cohort of girls (might a few of them learn about it, might they pay you an occasional visit?) whose nights in bed with their husbands would feel like proper compensation for their days of washing and ironing.

That future, that particular old age, however, refused to occur.

It had to do, most likely, with the accident (the backfiring car, the horse) that left you with that gimp leg. It had to do with the tiny apartment over the laundry (who expected rents to go up the way they did?), where the smell of mouse pellets and dry-cleaning chemicals seemed only to be made worse by the veils of perfume you sprayed around. What boy would want to come there?

It had to do as well with the surprising timidity of youth; the endangered-species status (or so it seemed) of the fearless princelings you remembered from your own early days—the boys (old men now, the ones who were still alive at all) who'd been drunk on confidence, touching in their unpracticed attempts at swagger. They'd been replaced by this generation of alarmingly well-behaved man-children, who seemed content to learn about women at the hands of girls who knew almost as little about their own bodies as the boys who fumbled with them.

Eventually, by the time you'd come to think of seventy as still young, you bought yourself a bit of real estate. It lay a considerable distance from town—who could afford even the outskirts, anymore? Once the deal had been struck you stood (aided by the cane you still couldn't quite believe you carried) on your modest patch of bare ground surrounded by forest, and decided that your house would be made of candy.

You did the research. It was, in fact, possible to construct bricks—out of sugar, glycerin, cornstarch, and a few unmentionable toxins—that would stand up to the rain. Gingerbread, if fortified with sufficient cement dust, would do as a roof.

The rest, of course, would require ongoing maintenance. The windows of spun sugar were good for a single winter, if that; the piped-on lintels and windowsills would need to be remade every spring, even when the icing was reinforced with Elmer's glue. The tiles made of lollipops, the specially ordered shafts of candy cane that served as banisters and railings, held up, but faded in the summer heat and had to be replaced. What could be more depressing than elderly-looking candy?

The house, however, was charming, in its insane and lav-
ishly reckless way, all the more so because it put out its lurid
colors, emanated its smells of sugar and ginger, in a tree-
shadowed glade far from even the most rudimentary of roads.

And then you waited.

You had—it was probably a miscalculation—expected a
more exploratory spirit among the local youngsters, whatever
their general devotion to decent behavior. Where were the
sweet little picnickers; where were the boy gangs looking for
hideouts where they could (with your approval) imbibe the
whiskey they needed in order to fully imagine themselves?
Where were the young lovers in search of secret sylvan places
they could claim as their own?

Time did not pass quickly. There wasn't much for you to
do. You found yourself replacing the frosting and lollipops
more often than necessary, simply because you needed proj-
ects, and because (it was a little crazy, but you didn't regret a
trace of craziness in yourself) you wondered if a heightened
version—a sharpening of cookie smell, some other manufac-
turer who produced candy with brighter stripes and swirls—
might make a difference.

As eighty approached, your first and only visitors were not
quite who you'd been expecting. They looked promising when
they first emerged, blinking with surprise, from among the
tree trunks into the little clearing in which your house stood.

They were sexy, the girl as well as the boy, with their starved
and foxy faces—that hungrily alert quality you see sometimes
in kids who've been knocked around a little. They were pierced

and tattooed. And they were, even more gratifyingly, ravenous. The boy didn't seem to mind that the handfuls of icing he stuffed into his mouth were so clearly held together with paste. The girl sucked seductively (with the cartoonish lewdness of girls taught by porn rather than experience) on a scarlet lollipop.

The boy said, through a mouthful of icing and Elmer's, "Hey, Grandma, what's up?"

The girl just smiled at him, tongue pressed to lollipop, as if he were clever and intoxicatingly dangerous; as if he were a rebel and a hero.

And what, exactly, did you expect those young psychopaths, those beaten children, to do, after they'd eaten half your house, without the remotest expression of wonder, or even of simple politeness? Were you surprised that they ransacked the place, eating their way from room to room, stopping every now and then to mock the bits of jewelry they found (she, with your pearls around her neck: "Our mother has pearls like these, how do you like them on me?") or the vase you'd had since your grandmother died, into which the boy took a long, noisy piss. Did you think they'd fail to complain, ultimately, that there seemed to be nothing here but candy to eat, that they needed a little protein as well?

Were you relieved, maybe just a little, when they lifted you up (you weighed almost nothing by then) and shoved you into the oven? Did it seem unanticipated but right, somehow—did it strike you as satisfying, as a fate finally realized—when they slammed the door behind you?

JACKED

This is not a smart boy we're talking about. This is not a kid who can be trusted to remember to take his mother to her chemo appointment, or to close the windows when it rains.

Never mind asking him to sell the cow, when he and his mother are out of cash, and the cow is their last asset.

We're talking about a boy who doesn't get halfway to town with his mother's sole remaining possession before he's sold the cow to some stranger for a handful of beans. The guy claims they're magic beans, and that, it seems, is enough for Jack. He doesn't even ask what variety of magic the beans supposedly deliver. Maybe they'll transform themselves into seven beautiful wives for him. Maybe they'll turn into the seven deadly sins, and buzz around him like flies for the rest of his life.

Jack isn't doubtful. Jack isn't big on questions. Jack is the boy who says, *Wow, dude, magic beans, really?*

There are any number of boys like Jack. Boys who prefer the crazy promise, the long shot, who insist that they're natural-born winners. They have a great idea for a screenplay—they just need, you know, someone to write it for them. They DJ at friends' parties, believing a club owner will wander in sooner or later and hire them to spin for multitudes. They drop out of vocational school because they can see, after a semester or two, that it's a direct path to loserdom—better to live in their childhood bedrooms, temporarily unemployed, until fame and prosperity arrive.

Is Jack's mother upset when he strides back into the house, holds out his hand, and shows her what he's gotten for the cow? She is.

What have I done, how exactly have all the sacrifices I've made, all the dinners I put together out of nothing and ate hardly any of myself, how exactly did I raise you to be this cavalier and unreliable, could you please explain that to me, please?

Is Jack disappointed by his mother's poverty of imagination, her lack of nerve in the face of life's gambles, her continued belief in the budget-conscious, off-brand caution that's gotten her exactly nowhere? He is.

I mean, Mom, look at this house. Don't you think thrift is some kind of death? Ask yourself. Since Dad died, why hasn't anyone come around? Not even Hungry Hank. Not even Half-Wit Willie.

Jack doesn't want, or need, to hear her answer, though it runs silently through her mind.

I have my beautiful boy, I see strong young shoulders bent over the washbasin every morning. What would I want with Hungry Hank's yellow teeth, or Half-Wit Willie's bent-up body?

Nevertheless, her son has sold the cow for a handful of

beans. Jack's mother tosses the beans out the window, and sends him to bed without supper.

Fairy tales are generally moral tales. In the bleaker version of this one, mother and son both starve to death.

That lesson would be: Mothers, try to be realistic about your imbecilic sons, no matter how charming their sly little grins, no matter how heartbreaking the dark-gold tousle of their hair. If you romanticize them, if you insist on virtues they clearly lack, if you persist in your blind desire to have raised a wise child, one who'll be helpful in your old age . . . don't be surprised if you find that you've fallen on the bathroom floor, and end up spending the night there, because he's out drinking with his friends until dawn.

That is not, however, the story of "Jack and the Beanstalk."

The implication of this particular tale is: Trust strangers. Believe in magic.

In "Jack and the Beanstalk," the stranger has not lied. The next morning, Jack's bedroom window is obscured by rampant green. He looks out into leaves the size of skillets, and a stalk as thick as an oak's trunk. When he cranes his neck upward, he sees that the beanstalk is so tall it vanishes into the clouds.

Right. Invest in desert real estate, where an interstate highway is certain to be built soon. Get in on the ground floor of your uncle's revolutionary new age-reversal system. Use half the grocery money to buy lottery tickets every week.

Jack, being Jack, does not ask questions, nor does he wonder if climbing the beanstalk is the best possible idea.

At the beanstalk's apex, on the upper side of the cloud-bank, he finds himself standing before a giant's castle, built on a particularly fleecy rise of cloud. The castle is dizzyingly white, prone to a hint of tremble, as if built of concentrated clouds; as if a proper rainstorm could reduce it to an enormous, pearly puddle.

Being Jack, he walks right up to the titanic snow-colored door. Who, after all, wouldn't be glad to see him?

Before he can knock, though, he hears his name called by a voice so soft it might merely be a gust of wind that's taught itself to say, *Jaaaaack.*

The wind coalesces into a cloud-girl; a maiden of the mist.

She tells Jack that the giant who lives in the castle killed Jack's father, years ago. The giant would have killed the infant Jack as well, but Jack's mother so ardently pled her case, holding the baby to her bosom, that the giant spared Jack, on the condition that Jack's mother never reveal the cause of his father's death.

Maybe that's why Jack's mother has always treated him as if he were bounty and hope, incarnate.

The mist-girl tells Jack that everything the giant owns belongs rightfully to him. Then she vanishes, as quickly as the wisp of an exhaled cigarette.

Jack, however, being Jack, had assumed already that everything the giant owns—everything everybody owns— rightfully belongs to him. And he'd never really believed that story about his father getting dysentery on a business trip to Brazil.

He raps on the door, which is opened by the giant's wife. The wife may once have been pretty, but no trace of loveliness remains. Her hair is thinning, her housecoat stained. She's as offhandedly careworn as a fifty-foot-tall version of Jack's mother.

Jack announces that he's hungry, that he comes from a place where the world fails to provide.

The giant's wife, who rarely receives visitors of any kind, is happy to see a handsome, miniature man-child standing at her door. She invites him in, feeds him breakfast, though she warns him that if her husband comes home, he'll eat *Jack* for breakfast.

Does Jack stick around anyway? Of course he does. Does the giant arrive home unexpectedly? He does.

He booms from the vastness of the hallway:

Fe fi fo fum
I smell the blood of an Englishman.
Be he alive or be he dead,
I'll grind his bones to make my bread.

The giant's wife conceals Jack in, of all places, the very saucepan in which her husband would cook him. She's barely got the lid put down when the giant lumbers in.

The giant is robustly corpulent, thundering, strident, dangerous in the way of barroom thugs, of any figure who is comical in theory (he wears a jerkin and tights) but truly threatening in fact, simply because he's fool enough and drunk enough to do serious harm; simply because he's a stranger to reason, because killing a man with a pool cue seems like a justifiable response to some vaguely insulting remark.

The giantess assures her husband that he merely smells the ox she's cooked him for lunch.

Really?

Here we move, briefly, into farce. There's nowhere else for us to go.

Giant: *I know what ox smells like. I know what the blood of an Englishman smells like.*

Giantess: *Well, this is a new kind of ox. It's flavored.*

Giant: *What?*

Giantess: *It's brand new. You can also get Tears of a Princess Ox. You can get Wicked Queen Envy Ox.*

She serves him the ox. A whole ox.

Giant: *Hm. Tastes like regular ox to me.*

Giantess: *Maybe I won't get this kind anymore.*

Giant: *There's nothing wrong with regular ox.*

Giantess: *But a little variety, every now and then . . .*

Giant: *You get suckered in too easily.*

Giantess: *I know. No one knows that better than I do.*

After the giant has eaten the ox, he commands his wife to bring him his bags of gold, so he can perform the day's tally. This is a ritual, a comforting reminder that he's just as rich today as he was yesterday, and the day before.

Once he's content that he still has all the gold he's ever
had, he lays his colossal head down on the tabletop and falls into
the kind of deep, wheezing nap anybody would want to take
after eating an ox.

Which is Jack's cue to climb back out of the saucepan, grab
the bags of gold, and take off.

And which would be the giantess's cue to resuscitate her
marriage. It would be the time for her to holler, "Thief," and
claim never to have seen Jack before.

By evening, she and her husband could have sat laughing
at the table, each holding aloft one of Jack's testicles on a tooth-
pick before popping them into their mouths. They could have
declared to each other, It's enough. It's enough to be rich, and
live on a cloud together; to age companionably; to want nothing more than they've got already.

The giant's wife seems to agree, however, that robbing her
husband is a good move.

We all know couples like this. Couples who've been wag-
ing the battle for decades; who seem to believe that if finally,
someday, one of them can prove the other wrong—deeply
wrong, soul-wrong—they'll be exonerated, and released. Amass-
ing the evidence, working toward the proof, can swallow an
entire life.

Jack and his mother, wealthy now (Jack's mother has invested
the gold in stocks and real estate), don't move to a better

neighborhood. They can't abandon the beanstalk. So they rebuild. Seven fireplaces, cathedral ceilings, indoor and outdoor pools.

They continue living together, mother and son. Jack doesn't date. Who knows what succession of girls and boys sneak in through the sliding glass doors at night, after the mother has sunk to the bottom of her own private lake, with the help of Absolut and Klonopin?

Jack and his mother are doing fine. Especially considering that, recently, they were down to their last cow.

But as we all know, it's never enough. No matter how much it is.

Jack and his mother still don't have a black American Express card. They don't have a private plane. They don't own an island.

And so, Jack goes up the beanstalk again. He knocks for a second time at the towering cloud-door.

The giantess answers again. She seems not to recognize Jack, and it's true that he's no longer dressed in the cheap lounge lizard outfit—the tight pants and synthetic shirt he boosted at the mall. He's all Marc Jacobs now. He has a shockingly expensive haircut.

But still. Does the giantess really believe a different, better-dressed boy has appeared at her door, one with the same sly grin and the same dark-gold hair, however improved the cut?

There is, after all, the well-known inclination to continue to sabotage our marriages, without ever leaving them. And there's this, too. There's the appeal of the young thief who robs you, and climbs back down off your cloud. It's possible to love that boy, in a wistful and hopeless way. It's possible to love his greed and narcissism, to grant him that which is beyond your own capacities: heedlessness, cockiness, a self-devotion so pure it borders on the divine.

The scenario plays itself out again. This time, when the fifty-foot-tall dim-witted thug *Fi fi fo fums*, early and unexpected, from the hallway, the giantess hides Jack in the oven.

We don't need advanced degrees to understand something about her habit of flirtation with eating Jack.

The second exchange between giant and giantess—the one about how he smells the blood of an Englishman, and she assures him it's just the bullock she's fixed for lunch—is too absurd even for farce.

Let's imagine an unconscious collusion between husband and wife, then. He knows something's up. He knows she's hiding something, or someone. Let's imagine he prefers a wife who's capable of deceit. A wife who can manage something more interesting than drudgery and peevish, drowsy fidelity.

This time, after polishing off the bullock, the giant demands to be shown the hen that lays golden eggs. And, a moment later, there she is: a prizewinning pullet, as regal and self-important as it's possible for a chicken to be. She stands before the giant, her claw–tipped, bluish feet firmly planted on the tabletop, and, with a low cackle of triumph, lays another golden egg.

Which the giant picks up and examines. It's the daily egg. They never vary. The giant, however, maintains his attachment to the revisiting of his own bounty, as he does to his postprandial snooze, face down on the tabletop, wheezing out blasts of bullock-reeking breath, emitting a lake of drool.

Again, Jack emerges (this time from the oven), and makes off with the hen. Again, the giantess watches him steal her husband's joy and fortune. Again, she adores the meanness of Jack, a small-time crook dressed now in two-hundred-dollar jeans. She envies him his rapaciousness, his insatiability. She who has let herself go, who prepares the meals and does the dishes and wanders, with no particular purpose, from room to room. She who finds herself strangely glad to be in the presence of someone avaricious and heartless and uncaring.

Are we surprised to learn that, a year or so later, Jack goes up the beanstalk one more time?

By now, there's nothing left for him and his mother to buy. They've got the car and driver, they've got the private plane, they own that small, otherwise-uninhabited island in the Lesser Antilles, where they've built a house that's staffed year-round, in anticipation of their single annual visit.

We always want more, though. Some of us want more than others, it's true, but we always want more of . . . something. More love, more youth, more . . .

On his third visit, Jack decides not to press his luck with the giantess. This time, he sneaks in through the back.

He finds the giant and giantess unaltered, though it would seem they've had to cut back, having lost their gold and their magic hen. The castle has dissolved a bit—sky knifes in through gaps in the cloud-walls. The daily lunch of an entire animal runs more along the lines of an antelope or an ibex, sinewy and dark-tasting, no longer the fattened, farm-tender ox or bullock of their salad days.

Still, habits resist change. The giant devours his creature, spits out horns and hooves, and demands his last remaining treasure: a magic harp.

The harp is a prize of a different order entirely. Who knows about its market value? It's nothing so simple as gold coins or golden eggs. It too is made of gold, but it's not prosaic in the way of actual currency.

It's a harp like any harp—strings, knee, neck, tuning pins— but its head is the head of a woman, slightly smaller than an apple, more stern than beautiful; more Athena than Botticelli Venus. And it can play itself.

The giant commands the harp to play. The harp obliges. It plays a tune unknown on the earth below; a melody that emanates from clouds and stars, a song of celestial movements, the music of the spheres, that which composers like Bach and Chopin came close to approximating but which, being ethereal, cannot be produced by instruments made of brass or wood, cannot be summoned by human breath or fingering.

The harp plays the giant into his nap. That gargantuan head makes its thudding daily contact with the tabletop.

What must the giantess think, when Jack creeps in and

grabs the harp? *Again? You're kidding. You actually want the very last of our treasures?*

Is she appalled, or relieved, or both? Does she experience some ecstasy of total loss? Or has she had enough? Is she going to put an end, at last, to Jack's voracity?

We'll never know. Because it's the harp, not the giantess, who finally protests. As Jack makes for the door, the harp calls out, "Master, help me, I'm being stolen."

The giant wakes, looks around uncertainly. He's been dreaming. Can this be his life, his kitchen, his haggard and grudging wife?

By the time he's up and after Jack, Jack has already traversed the cloud-field and reached the top of the beanstalk, holding firm to the harp as the harp cries out for rescue.

It's a race down the beanstalk. Jack is hampered by his grip on the harp—he can only climb one-handed—but the giant has far more trouble than Jack in negotiating the stalk itself, which, for the giant, is thin and unsteady, like the rope he was forced to climb in gym class when he was a weepy, lonely boy.

As Jack nears the ground, he calls to his mother to bring him an axe. He's lucky—she's semi-sober today. She rushes out with an axe. Jack chops the beanstalk down, while the giant is still as high as a hawk circling for rabbits.

The beanstalk falls like a redwood. The giant hits the earth so hard his body crashes through the topsoil, imbeds itself ten feet deep, leaves a giant-shaped chasm in the middle of a cornfield.

It's a mercy, of sorts. What, after all, did the giant have left, with his gold and his hen and his harp all gone?

Jack has had the giant-hole filled in, right over the giant's body, and in a rare act of piety he's ordered a grove of lilac bushes planted over the giant's resting-place. If you were to look down at the lilac grove from above, you'd see that it's shaped like an enormous man, arms and legs akimbo; a man frozen in an attitude of oddly voluptuous surrender.

Jack and his mother prosper. Jack, in his rare moments of self-questioning, remembers what the mist-girl told him, years earlier. The giant committed a crime. Jack has, since infancy, been entitled to everything the giant owned. This salves the stripling conscience that's been growing feebly within Jack as he's gotten older.

Jack's mother has started collecting handbags (she especially prizes her limited-edition Murakami Cherry Blossom by Louis Vuitton), and meeting her girlfriends for lunches that can go on until four or five p.m. Jack sometimes acquires girls and boys in neighboring towns, sometimes rents them, but always arranges for them to arrive late at night, in secret. Jack is not, as we know, the brightest bulb on the Christmas tree, but he's canny enough to understand that only his mother will uncritically adore him forever; that if one of the girls or boys were suffered to stay, the fits of mysterious frustration, the critiques, would set in soon enough.

The hen, who cares only for the eggs she produces, lays a gold one every day, and lives contentedly in her concrete coop with her twenty-four-hour guard, Jack's attempt at exterminating all the local foxes having proven futile.

Only the harp is restive and sorrowful. Only the harp looks yearningly out through the window of the room in which it resides, a room that affords it a view of the lilac grove planted over the giant's imbedded body. The harp, long mute, dreams of the time when it lived on a cloud and played music too beautiful for anyone but the giant to hear.

POISONED

ou wanted to last night.

And tonight, I don't think I want to.

Why, exactly, is that?

It's weird. Don't you think it's at least a little bit weird? And I'm, well, getting tired of it.

When exactly did you change your mind?

I didn't. Okay, I'm tired of pretending that I'm not tired of doing it.

Is it because of that apple joke, today at the market? Did that bother you?

Hell no. You think I'm not used to apple jokes by now?

You've always told me you liked it. So, you've been lying?

No. Well, not exactly lying. I suppose I've liked it because you like it so much. But it seems that tonight, I don't really want to.

That's a little ever so slightly humiliating, don't you think? For me, I mean.

No. I've been doing it because I love you. When you love somebody, it makes you happy to make him happy.

Even if you think it's weird. Even if you think it's disgusting.

I didn't say disgusting. "Weird" and "disgusting" are not synonyms.

You didn't get tired of doing it for the midgets.

They weren't midgets. They were *dwarfs*. I don't know why you refuse to understand the difference.

Sorry. I'm sorry. I'm displacing my emotions.

You got that phrase from your shrink, do you even know what it means?

I'm sorry about the *dwarfs*. I know you loved them.

Or I loved it that they loved me, I've never been completely sure.

Do you think we should have them over again?

Because it was so much fun the last time?

I wouldn't say it was *un*fun. Did you think it was?

You had to lift them up to get them into our chairs. Our spoons were the size of spades to them. Have you really actually forgotten that?

I was trying to be kind. I was trying to be hostly. I took away the love of their goddamned lives. Did my position that night strike you as easy?

No. You were trying to be generous to them. I know that. I do.

Okay. Ten minutes. Just ten, okay?

This really matters to you, doesn't it?

Please don't condescend.

Could you tell me something to say that won't offend you?

It matters to me. Okay, right, I'm a little ever so slightly embarrassed that it matters to me. But it does.

Tell me something you love about me.

Come on.

Be specific.

Okay. I love the thing you do with your mouth when you're concentrating. This little squinchy thing, sort of half biting your lip but not exactly, it's just . . . squinchy, it's totally involuntary, it's so you.

Tell me another.

I love it when I wake up before you do, and then when you wake up you have this kind of pure astonished awed expression, like you can't quite believe you're . . . where you are. It fucks with me. It's what gives me those morning hard-ons.

Okay. Ten minutes.

Are you sure?

Does it bother you, that I like making you happy?

Ten minutes, then.

Hey, I'll go to twelve. For you.

I adore you.

Be careful with the lid, all right?

Aren't I always careful with the lid?

Yes. I'm honestly not sure why I said that.

Are you all right? Is this comfortable?

I am. It is.

Do you think . . .

What?

I feel like some kind of creep, now.

Just tell me.

Do you think you could cross your hands just a little lower down? More like directly over your breasts?

Mm-hm.

Yeah. Perfect. That's so entirely completely perfect.

I'm closing my eyes now. I'm going into the zone.

God, you're beautiful.

I wish sometimes I could watch you. Watching me.

I'd like that, too. But it wouldn't . . .

Of course it wouldn't.

Look at your skin. Look at your lips. Look at the petals of your eyelids.

I'm going to stop talking now. You can lower the lid.

I'm the luckiest man in the world.

I'm not talking anymore. I'm going into the zone.

Twelve minutes, tops. I promise.

Shh.

Twelve minutes on the dot. Promise. Thank you for doing this, I know you're stopping speaking. But, well, thank you. It matters to me, it does. Okay. Twelve minutes and I lay one on you. Then we can order in, okay? Or we can go out, whatever you like. We could catch a movie. But thank you for twelve minutes. I mean, look at you. Sleep like death. Before I even existed. For you, I mean. When I was, okay, I like thinking this way, when I was a dream you were having, when I was a

premonition, when I was perfect because I didn't exist, when I was pure possibility, and, I really hope this isn't weird, when you were immaculate, and entirely strange, and the most perfect and beautiful creature I'd ever seen. Before I lifted the lid, I mean, and kissed you for the first time.

A MONKEY'S PAW

Take the Whites, a modest but happy family. A happy-enough family. It's just the three of them: mother, father, and son. The son works in the local factory. If he's cross about supporting his parents; if he chafes at his sexless nights or wonders about a youth devoid of carousing and petty criminality; if he's upset about certain premature afflictions brought on by his labors (that tricky knee, the painful knot at the base of his spine) at the age of twenty-two, he never brings it up. He was not born into a place or time when sons kiss their parents goodbye, gently chide their mother's hanky-dabbed tears, and stride off into lives of their own.

They live in a cottage, though it's not the thatched, tidy dwelling the word "cottage" ordinarily brings to mind. It sags in a slushy, wind-haunted remoteness. The Whites have not been offered much in the way of choices.

And yet, they don't bicker. They don't get snappish over minor domestic failings. These quarters cramped and damp, this road rendered impassible by mud more than half the year, strike them as inevitable, and they console themselves with vague references to how it could have been worse (although it's difficult to say what "worse" might entail). There is no hint among them of *Why did I let you bring me here?* or *When will you die, so I can escape?*

The visitor who arrives one mucky night is not a stranger; or not exactly a stranger, though he is in fact strange. He's an old friend of Mr. White's, a man who, when young, was prone (more so than Mr. White) to wild and defiant inclinations. In the way of certain trouble-prone boys, he eventually joined the army. He's been away on military errands for more than two decades, most recently in India. He's spent the last twenty years helmeted, taciturn, a defender of the Empire, in realms of superstition, of blessings and curses, of darkly magical acts that are usually faked but can seem, on occasion, to be not exactly genuine, but . . . other than counterfeit, as well.

The visitor brings with him a gift, the severed paw of a monkey, which he claims has the power to grant three wishes.

The Whites are unsure about how to receive this particular present. They could use three wishes—a single wish would be riches beyond calculation. But, really. This gruesome, withered little thing, its dead, brown-black fingers curled into themselves? It would seem that Mr. White's old friend has lost his mind, which is not unusual among men who've been long in strange and remote places.

Still, it'd be impolite to refuse it. Right?

Mr. White takes the paw into his own hand, and is astonished and appalled when it convulses, ever so slightly, upon contact with the flesh of his own palm.

Before he can cry out, though, the visitor has snatched it back. He says, in an unsteady voice, that he was about to commit a crime. He's been unable to rid himself of the paw, he'd thought he could free himself by giving it to a poor, innocent family . . .

The Whites just stare at him. What is there to say?

The visitor tells them he bemoans the day he ever laid tired eyes on the monkey's paw.

With a spasm of lunatic resolve, he throws it into the fireplace.

Mr. White just as quickly retrieves it, singeing his own fingertips. He's embarrassed for his friend. He assures him that a gift is a gift. He says he's always been drawn to exotica, and there's not much of that in this neighborhood.

The visitor, looking gaunt and terrified as a muskrat in a trap, stumbles to the door. Before taking his leave, he warns the Whites not to wish on the paw, and implores them, should they find themselves wish-prone, to restrict their requests to the most sensible possible desires.

Then he's out the door. The rain absorbs him back into the night.

Mother and son are quick to render their verdict. They break out in gusts of laughter.

Sensible wishes? Please send us a new dustpan? Grant us, if you will, fewer roaches in the larder?

Mr. White remains silent. He closes the door, through which rain is blowing like a swarm of hornets.

He could swear he felt the paw clench when it was given

to him. He's holding it again, though, and it's inert as death itself.

Mr. White can manage only a muted protest on the poor man's behalf. "He's been harmed by too much strangeness, you didn't know us when we were boys . . ."

Mrs. White snatches the paw from him, mutters an invented incantation, and says, "I wish . . ."

She pauses. She claims she has nothing to wish for (she who washes dishes in an old iron pot, who does her best to coax fires out of soggy logs).

"I wish for two hundred pounds," she says eventually, two hundred pounds being the sum still owed on the cottage. With two hundred pounds, this warren of dim, low-ceilinged dankness could be theirs.

A more sensible wish is difficult to imagine.

Nothing happens. No wad of bank notes manifests itself in the sugar bowl, no coins rattle down the flue.

They take themselves off to bed.

Once Mr. and Mrs. White are settled under the quilts together, she does not wonder, even as sleep descends, why she married a man who'd convey her, after their modest village wedding, to a place like this. (Should she have guessed, when he appeared at their marriage ceremony in his father's mothballed suit, when he insisted that a carriage was a needless expense?) Mr. White, a troubled sleeper, does not inquire inwardly, as he turns this way and that, trying to find a sleep-friendly position, about his choice of a wife so lacking in ambition or faith. He does not ask himself, Why would full ownership of this hovel so much as cross her mind, even in jest?

The next morning, the son leaves for work. By late afternoon, a representative of the factory arrives to inform Mr. and Mrs. White that there's been an accident. Their son has been snatched up by his machine, as if he were the raw material for some product made of manglement, of bone shards and snapped sinews, of blood-spray that turned quickly, before the eyes of the other workers, from red to black.

The man from the factory is appropriately, professionally sympathetic. He knows there's no compensation for a loss like this. The factory owners do, however, maintain a practice of paying the families of the men who are, on occasion, taken by the machines. It's not much, God knows, but the company is prepared to offer the following sum of money to the boy's parents . . .

You do not, of course, need me to tell you the actual figure.

Nor do you need me to tell you—certainly not in detail—about the boy's grief-deranged mother, who made the wish in the first place; about how she, late one night—several days after what remains of her son has been sealed into its box (there was no viewing of the body), after the box has been interred in the weedy churchyard—takes up the monkey's paw and calls, into the empty parlor, into the rain beyond the parlor, "Bring him back."

Nothing happens.

Nothing happens immediately.

It takes several hours for the Whites, after they've gone to bed, to hear the sound of approaching footsteps, coming from outside. It takes only moments, however, for them to realize that the footsteps possess a measured slowness, an aspect of drag, as if each step did not involve boot-sole leaving the surface of the ground and so has to be painfully gained, a slide through the sludge, before the next step can be negotiated.

Both of them understand it at the same moment. It's a long walk from the cemetery.

Mrs. White rushes down the narrow stairs, with Mr. White behind her.

"He's back!" she declares.

He can barely bring himself to respond. "*It's* back."

The mauled corpse, the creature made now of shattered bone and crushed mask of a face (the creature who had once toddled giggling after a rubber ball, who had skated cheerfully on ponds with its friends) is back. It is, even now, creaking through the garden gate.

It has been summoned. It still recognizes the light in the window.

As Mrs. White struggles to unbolt the door, Mr. White takes up the monkey's paw. He's prepared to shout, "Make it go away."

And yet, he remains silent. He knows what he should do. But he can't bear the idea of his wife throwing open the door and finding nothing but wind outside. He's not sure he could survive the sorrow and fury she'd aim at him when she turned back from the empty threshold.

So Mr. White stands in the middle of the room, holding the monkey's paw tightly in his hand, as his wife throws the door open, as he and his wife behold what stands before them, expecting to be welcomed in.

They have lived together now, the three of them, for more than a year. The creature sprawls, during the days, in the up-holstered chair, beside whatever flicker of fire has been coaxed from the wet logs. When night arrives, the creature hauls itself wordlessly upstairs, clumping on each tread, where it remains in its bedroom (there's no telling whether it sleeps) until morning comes again, when it resumes its place at the fireside.

Still, it is their child. What's left of him. The Whites have covered the parlor walls with every old photograph they have: their son tiny in a snowsuit, grinning among a swirl of wind-blown white flakes; their son somberly adolescent in a bow tie, posing for the school's photographer; their son smiling nervously beside the unsuitable girl (the hefty one, sly-eyed and morally slack, who is now the drunken wife of the town butcher) he took to his first dance.

The Whites burn incense to cover the smell. When spring arrives, they fill the house with lilacs and roses.

Mr. and Mrs. manage, as best they can, a version of their former days. They joke and reminisce. Mrs. White produces a mutton stew every Friday, although the creature no longer wants, or needs, to eat.

Usually, it stares blankly at the struggling fire, though every now and then, when some conversation has been broached, when Mother or Father asks if it wouldn't like another pillow, wonders if it remembers that trip they took, years ago, to that lake in the mountains, it raises what remains of its head, and trains on them its single, opaquely opalescent eyeball, with an expression not so much of anger as confusion. What crime has it committed? Its jailers are kind enough, they make their attempts at offering comfort, but why do they keep it here, what exactly did it do that was so wrong?

Days pass into nights, and nights into days. Nothing changes, either within the house or outside, where gray skies and the bare branches of trees drop their reflections into the puddles on the road.

The effort required to continue in this altered world shows, however. Mrs. White, on more than one evening, wonders wistfully over the whereabouts of Tom Barkin, the man she might have married, and the fact that the words "might have married" mean only that she was (as Mr. White points out) one of a dozen girls with whom Tom Barkin flirted shamelessly, seems to strengthen rather than deter her convictions about renounced possibility. Mr. White finally tells her he does not like, has never liked, her habit of whistling as she goes about her duties, but finds afterward that her grudgingly obedient cessation produces a strangled silence worse than the whistling had been. The undercooked bacon is no longer consumed by

Mr. White without comment. His infrequent baths no longer produce assurances that there's something nice about a man's natural smell. His stories are more often suffered, by Mrs. White, with an undisguised glaze of boredom.

The creature that sits staring into the smoking and smoldering logs appears to take no notice.

Mr. and Mrs. White remind themselves: This is still their son. They stand by him, as they must. They have that, at least, by way of virtue. They willed him into being, not once, but twice.

And so, the fire is kept alive. The stew is prepared every Friday. The occasional visitor is discouraged—the Whites are, they claim, simply too busy to receive, these days. There are moments, though, when Mrs. White imagines how much easier her life would be if Mr. White were to die of his compromised heart, and launch her into the simpler realm of widowhood, where nobody minds about whistling, or how the bacon is cooked; where Mr. White's sour, sweaty pungency would evaporate; where she would not be asked to feign amusement over the same story, told one more time. There are moments when Mr. White imagines his wife going away with Tom Barkin, who's old now, who's lost half his teeth, who still flirts with girls even as they recoil in horror. She'd be an adulteress, and no one would blame him for maintaining a determinedly cheerful demeanor in his solitude. He'd be a figure of sympathy. An acquaintance or two might even venture the long-withheld opinion that, as everyone in the village agrees, Mr. White really could have done better. And there are a few youngish local widows who don't seem like the kind of women who'd object to a man's smell, or wouldn't appreciate a rousing, well-told tale.

It would be easier, it seems, if there were fewer of them on the premises.

The Whites, all three of them, know exactly where the monkey's paw resides—on the top shelf of the cupboard, beside the cracked mixing bowl. They know, they always know, all of them know, it has one more wish to grant.

LITTLE MAN

hat if you had a child?

If you had a child, your job would be more than getting through the various holiday rushes, and wondering exactly how insane Mrs. Witters in Accounts Payable is going to be on any given day. It'd be about procuring tiny shoes and pull-toys and dental checkups; it'd be about paying into a college fund.

The unextraordinary house to which you return nightly? It'd be someone's future ur-house. It'd be the place—decades hence—someone will remember forever, a seat of comfort and succor, its rooms rendered larger and grander, exalted, by memory. This sofa, those lamps, purchased in a hurry, deemed good enough for now, then (they seem to be here still, years later): they'd be legendary, to someone.

Imagine reaching the point at which you want a child more than you can remember wanting anything else.

Having a child is not, however, anything like ordering a pizza. All the more so if you're a malformed, dwarfish man whose occupation, were you forced to name one, would be . . . What would you call yourself? A goblin? An imp? Adoption agencies are reluctant about *doctors* and *lawyers*, if they're single and over forty. So go ahead. Apply to adopt an infant as a two-hundred-year-old gnome.

You are driven slightly insane—you try to talk yourself down, it works some nights better than others—by the fact that for so much of the population, children simply . . . appear. Bing bang boom. A single act of love and, nine months later, this flowering, as mindless and senseless as a crocus bursting out of a bulb.

It's one thing to envy wealth and beauty and other gifts that seem to have been granted to others, but not you, by obscure but inarguable givers. It's another thing entirely to yearn for what's so readily available to any drunk and barmaid who link up for three minutes in one of the darker corners of any dank and scrofulous pub.

You listen carefully, then, when you hear the rumor. Some impoverished miller, a man whose business is going under (the small mill-owners, the ones who grind by hand, are vanishing—their flour and meal cost twice what the corporations can churn out, and the big-brand product is free of the gritty bits that find their way into a sack of flour no matter how careful you are); a man who hasn't got health insurance or investments, who hasn't been putting money into a pension (he's needed every cent just to keep the mill open).

That man has told the king his daughter can spin straw into gold.

The miller must have felt driven to it. He must have thought he needed a claim that outrageous if he was going to attract the attention of the king at all.

You suppose (as an aspiring parent yourself, you prefer to think of other parents as un-deranged) he hopes that if he can get his daughter into the palace, if he can figure out a way for her to meet the king, the king will be so smitten (doesn't every father believe his daughter to be irresistible?) that he'll forget about the absurd straw-into-gold story, after he's seen the pale grace of the girl's neck; after she's aimed that smile at him; after he's heard the sweet clarinet tone of her soft but surprisingly sonorous voice.

The miller apparently was unable to imagine all the pale-necked, shyly smiling girls the king has met already. Like most fathers, it's inconceivable to him that his daughter may not be singular; that she may be lovely and funny and smart, but not so much more so as to obliterate all the other contending girls.

The miller, poor foolish doting father that he is, never expected his daughter to get locked into a room full of straw, and commanded to spin it all into gold by morning, any more than most fathers expect their daughters to be un-sought-after by boys, or rejected by colleges, or abused by the men they eventually marry. Such notions don't appear on the spectrum of paternal possibility.

It gets worse.

The king, who really hates being fooled, announces, from

the doorway of the cellar room filled with straw, that if the girl hasn't spun it all into gold by morning, he'll have her executed.

What? Wait a minute . . .

The miller starts to confess, to beg forgiveness. He was joking; no, he was sinfully proud, he wanted his daughter to meet the king, he was worried about her future; I mean, your majesty, you can't be thinking of *killing* her . . .

The king looks glacially at the miller, has a guard escort him away, and withdraws, locking the door behind him.

Here's where you come in.

You're descended from a long line of minor wizards. Your people have, for generations, been able to summon rain, exorcise poltergeists, find lost wedding rings.

No one in the family, not over the last few centuries at any rate, has thought of making a living at it. It's not . . . respectable. It smells of desperation. And—as is the way with spells and conjurings—it's not one hundred percent reliable. It's an art, not a science. Who wants to refund a farmer's money as he stands destitute in his still-parched fields? Who wants to say, *I'm sorry, it works most of the time*, to the elderly couple who still hear cackles of laughter coming from under their mattress, whose cutlery still jumps up from the dinner table and flies around the room?

When you hear the story about the girl who can supposedly spin straw into gold (it's the talk of the kingdom), you don't immediately think, *This might be a way for me to get a child.* That would be too many steps down the line for most people, and you, though you have a potent heart and ferocity of intention, are not a particularly serious thinker. You work more from instinct. It's instinct, then, that tells you, *Help this girl, good might come of it.* Maybe simply because you, and you alone, have something to offer her. You who've never before had much to offer any of the girls who passed by, laughing with their boyfriends, leaving traces of perfume in their wake; perfume and powder and a quickening of the air they so recently occupied.

Spinning straw into gold is beyond your current capabilities, but not necessarily impossible to learn. There are ancient texts. There's your Aunt Farfalee, older than some of the texts but still alive, as far as you know; the only truly gifted member of your ragtag cohort, who are more generally prone to making rats speak in Flemish, or summoning beetles out of other people's Christmas pies.

Castles are easy to penetrate. Most people don't know that; most people think of them as fortified, impregnable. Castles, however, have been remodeled and revised, over and over again, by countless generations. There was the child-king who insisted on secret passageways, with peepholes that opened through the eyes of the ancestral portraits. There was the paranoid king who had escape tunnels dug, miles of them, opening out into woods, country lanes, and graveyards.

The girl, however, is surprised and impressed when you

materialize in the chamber full of straw. It has nothing to do with magic. Already, though, you've got credibility.

At first glance you see why the miller thought his gamble might work. She's a true beauty, slightly unorthodox, in the way of most great beauties. Her skin is smooth and poreless as pale pink china, her nose ever so slightly longer than it should be, her brown-black eyes wide-set, sable-lashed, all but quivering with curiosity, with depths.

She stares at you. She doesn't speak. Her life, starting this morning, has become so strange to her (she who yesterday was sewing grain sacks and sweeping stray corn kernels from the floor) that the sudden appearance of a twisted and stub-footed man, just under four feet tall, with a chin as long as a turnip, seems like merely another in the new string of impossibilities.

You tell her you're there to help. She nods her thanks. You get to work.

It doesn't go well, at first. The straw, run through the spinning wheel, comes out simply as straw, shredded and bent.

You refuse to panic, though. You repeat, silently, the spell taught to you by Aunt Farfalee (who is by now no bigger than a badger, with blank white eyes and fingers thin and stiff as icicles). You concentrate—belief is crucial. One of the reasons ordinary people are incapable of magic is simple dearth of conviction.

And, eventually . . . yes. The first few stalks are only touched with gold, like eroded relics, but the next are more gold than straw, and soon enough the wheel is spitting them out, strand upon strand of pure golden straw, deep in color, not the hard yellow of some gold but a yellow suffused with pink, ever so slightly incandescent in the torchlit room.

You both—you and the girl—watch, enraptured, as the piles of straw dwindle and masses of golden strands skitter onto the limestone floor. It's the closest you've come, yet, to love, to lovemaking—you at the spinning wheel with the girl behind you (she forgetfully puts her hand, gently, on your shoulder), watching in shared astonishment as the straw is spun into gold.

When it's all finished, she says, "My lord."

You're not sure whether she's referring to you or to God.

"Glad to be of service," you answer. "I should go, now."

"Let me give you something."

"No need."

But still, she takes a strand of beads from her neck, and holds them out to you. They're garnets, cheap, probably dyed, though in this room, at this moment, with all that golden straw emanating its faint light, they're as potently red-black as heart's blood.

She says, "My father gave me these for my eighteenth birthday."

She drapes the necklace over your head. An awkward moment occurs, when the beads catch on your chin, but the girl lifts them off, and her fingertips brush against your face. The strand of beads falls onto your chest. Onto the declivity where, were you a normal man, your chest would be.

"Thank you," she says.

You bow and depart. She sees you slipping away through the secret door, devoid of hinges or knob, one of the many commanded by the long-dead paranoid king.

"That's not magic," she laughs.

"No," you answer. "But magic is sometimes all about knowing where the secret door is, and how to open it."

With that, you're gone.

You hear about it the next day, as you walk along the edges of town, wearing the strand of garnets under your stained woolen shirt.

The girl pulled it off. She spun the straw into gold.

The king's response? Do it again tonight, in a bigger room, with twice as much straw.

He's joking. Right?

He's not joking. This, after all, is the king who passed the law about putting trousers on cats and dogs, who made too-loud laughter a punishable crime. According to rumor, he was abused by his father, the last king. But that's the story people always tell, isn't it, when they want to explain inexplicable behavior?

You do it again that night. The spinning is effortless by now. As you spin, you perform little comic flourishes for the girl. You spin for a while one-handed. You spin with your back to the wheel. You spin with your eyes closed.

She laughs and claps her hands. Her laughter is low and sonorous, like the sound of a clarinet.

This time, when you've finished, she gives you a ring. It, too, is cheap—silver, with a speck of diamond sunk into it.

She says, "This was my mother's."

She slips it onto your pinkie. It fits, just barely. You stand for a moment, staring at your own hand, which is not by any standards a pretty sight, with its knobbed knuckles and thick, yellowed nails. But here it is, your hand, with her ring on one of its fingers.

You slip away without speaking. You're afraid that anything you might say would be embarrassingly earnest.

The next day . . .

Right. One last roomful of straw, twice the size again. The king promises that this is the last, but insists on this third and final act of alchemy. He believes, it seems, that value resides in threes, which would explain the three garish and unnecessary towers he's had plunked onto the castle walls, the three advisers to whom he never listens, the three annual parades in commemoration of nothing in particular beyond the celebration of the king himself.

And . . .

If the girl pulls it off one more time, the king has announced he'll marry her, make her his queen.

That's the reward? Marriage to a man who'd have had you decapitated if you'd failed to produce not just one but three miracles?

Surely the girl will refuse.

You go to the castle one more time and do it again. It seems that it should be routine by now, the sight of the golden straw piling up, the fiery gleam of it, but somehow repetition hasn't rendered it commonplace. It is (or so you imagine) a little like being in love; like wondering anew, every morning, over the outwardly unremarkable fact that your lover is there, in bed beside you, about to open her eyes, and that, every morning, your face will be the first thing she sees.

When you've finished, she says, "I'm afraid I have nothing more to give you."

You pause. You're shocked to realize that you want something more from her. You've told yourself, the past two nights, that the necklace and the ring are marvels, but extraneous acts of gratitude; that you'd have done what you've done for nothing more than the sight of her thankful face.

It's surprising, then, that on this final night, you don't want to leave unrewarded. That you desire, with upsetting urgency, another token, a talisman, a further piece of evidence. Maybe it's because you know you won't see her again.

You say, "You aren't going to marry him, are you?"

She looks down at the floor, which is littered with stray strands of golden straw.

She says, "I'd be queen."

"But you'd be married to him. That would be the man who was going to kill you if you didn't produce the goods."

She lifts her head and looks at you.

"My father could live in the palace with me."

"And yet. You can't marry a monster."

"My father would live in the castle. The king's physicians would attend to him. He's ill, grain dust gets into your lungs."

You're as surprised as she is when you hear yourself say, "Promise me your firstborn child, then."

She merely blinks in astonishment, by way of an answer.

You've said it, though. You might as well forge on.

"Let me raise your first child," you say. "I'll be a good father, I'll teach the child magic, I'll teach the child generosity and forgiveness. The king isn't going to be much along those lines, don't you think?"

"If I refuse," she says, "will you expose me?"

Oh.

You don't want to descend to blackmail. You wish she hadn't posed the question, and you have no idea about how to answer. You'd never expose her. But you're so sure about your ability to rescue the still-unconceived child, who will, without your help, be abused by the father (don't men who've been abused always do the same to their children?), who'll become another punishing and capricious king in his own time, who'll demand meaningless parades and still-gaudier towers and who knows what else.

She interprets your silence as a yes. Yes, you'll turn her in if she doesn't promise the child to you.

She says, "All right, then. I promise to give you my first-born child."

You could take it back. You could tell her you were kidding, you'd never take a woman's child.

But you find—surprise—that you like this capitulation from her, this helpless acceding, from the most recent embodiment of all the girls over all the years who've given you nothing, not even a curious glance.

Welcome to the darker side of love.

You leave again without speaking. This time, though, it's not from fear of embarrassment. This time it's because you're greedy and ashamed, it's because you want the child, you need the child, and yet you can't bear to be yourself at this moment; you can't stand there any longer, enjoying your mastery over her.

The royal wedding takes place. Suddenly this common girl, this miller's daughter, is a celebrity; suddenly her face emblazons everything from banners to souvenir coffee mugs.

And she looks like a queen. Her glowy pallor, her dark intelligent eyes, are every bit as royal-looking as they need to be.

A year later, when the little boy is born, you go to the palace.

You've thought of letting it pass—of course you have—but after those nights of sleepless wondering over the life ahead, the return to the amplified solitude and hopelessness in which you've lived for the past year (people have tried to sell you key chains and medallions with the girl's face on them, assuming, as well they might, that you're just another customer; you, who wear the string of garnets under your shirts, who wear the silver ring on your finger) . . .

You can't let it pass after the bouts of self-torture about the confines of your face and body. Until those nights of spinning, no girl has ever let you get close enough for you to realize that you're possessed of wit and allure and compassion, that you'd be coveted, you'd be sought-after, if you were just . . .

Neither Aunt Farfalee nor the oldest and most revered of the texts has anything to say about transforming gnomes into straight-spined, striking men. Aunt Farfalee told you, in the low, rattling sigh that was once her voice, that magic has its limits; that the flesh has proven consistently, over centuries, vulnerable to afflictions but never, not even for the most potent of wizards, subject to improvement.

You go to the palace.

It's not hard to get an audience with the king and queen. One of the traditions, a custom so old and entrenched that even this king dare not abolish it, is the weekly Wednesday audience, at which any citizen who wishes to can appear in the throne room and register a complaint, after the king has taken a wife.

You are not the first in line. You wait as a corpulent young woman reports that a coven of witches in her district is causing the goats to walk on their hind legs, and saunter inside as if they owned the place. You wait as an old man objects to the new tax being levied on every denizen who lives past the age of eighty, which is the king's way of claiming as his own that which would otherwise be passed along to his subjects' heirs.

As you stand in line, you see that the queen sees you.

She looks entirely natural on the throne, every bit as much

as does her image on banners and mugs and key chains. She's noticed you, but nothing changes in her expression. She listens with the customary feigned attention to the woman whose goats are sitting down to dinner with the family, to the man who doesn't want his fortune sucked away before he dies. It's widely known that these audiences with king and queen never produce results of any kind. Still, people want to come and be heard.

As you wait, you notice the girl's father, the miller (the former miller), seated among the members of court, in a three-cornered hat and ermine collar. He regards the line of assembled supplicants with a dowager aunt's indignity; with an expression of superiority and sentimental piety—the recently bankrupt man who gambled with his daughter's life, and happens, thanks to you, to have won.

When your turn arrives, you bow to queen and king. The king nods his traditional, absentminded acknowledgment. His head might have been carved from marble. His eyes are ice-blue under the rim of his gem-encrusted crown. He might already be, in life, the stone version that will top his sarcophagus.

You say, "My queen, I think you know what I've come for."

The king looks disapprovingly at his wife. His face bears no hint of question. He skips over the possibility of innocence. He only wonders what, exactly, it is she must have done.

The queen nods. You can't tell what's going through her mind. She's learned, apparently, during the past year, how to evince an expression of royal opacity, which she did not possess when you were spinning the straw into gold for her.

She says, "Please reconsider."

You're not about to reconsider. You might have considered reconsidering before you found yourself in the presence of these two, this tyrannical and ignorant monarch and the girl who agreed to marry him.

You tell her that a promise was made. You leave it at that. She glances over at the king, and can't conceal a moment of miller's-daughter nervousness.

She turns to you again. She says, "This is awkward, isn't it?"

You waver. You're assaulted by conflicting emotions. You understand the position she's in. You care for her. You're in love with her. It's probably the hopeless ferocity of your love that impels you to stand firm, to refuse her refusal—she who has on one hand succeeded spectacularly and, on the other, consented to what has to be, at best, a cold and brutal marriage. You can't simply relent and walk back out of the room. You can't bring yourself to be so debased.

She doesn't care for you, after all. You're someone who did her a favor, once. She doesn't even know your name.

With that thought, you decide to offer a compromise.

You tell her she has three days to guess your name, in the general spirit of her husband's fixation on threes. If she can accomplish that, if she can guess your name within the next three days, the deal's off.

If she can't . . .

You do not of course say this aloud, but if she can't, you'll raise the child in a forest glade. You'll teach him the botanical names of the trees, and the secret names of the animals.

You'll instruct him in the arts of mercy and patience. And you'll see, in the boy, certain of her aspects—the great dark pools of her eyes, maybe, or her slightly exaggerated, aristocratic nose.

The queen nods in agreement. The king scowls. He can't, however, ask questions, not here, not with his subjects lined up before him. He can't appear to be baffled, underinformed, misused.

You bow again and, as straight-backed as your torqued spine will allow it, you back out of the throne room.

You'll never know what went on between queen and king once they were alone together. You hope she confessed everything, and insisted that a vow, once made, can't be broken. You even go so far as to imagine she might defend you for your offer of a possible reprieve.

You suspect, though, that she still feels endangered; that she can't be sure her husband will forgive her for allowing him to believe she herself had spun the straw into gold. Having produced a male heir she has now, after all, rendered herself dispensable. And so, when confronted, she probably came up with . . . some tale of spells and curses, some fabrication in which you, a hobgoblin, are entirely to blame.

You wish you could feel more purely angry about that possibility. You wish you didn't sympathize, not even a little, with her, in the predicament she's created for herself.

This, then, is love. This is the experience from which

you've felt exiled for so long. This rage mixed up with empathy; this simultaneous desire for admiration and victory.

You wish you found it more unpleasant. Or, at any rate, you wish you found it as unpleasant as it actually is.

The queen sends messengers out all over the kingdom, in an attempt to track down your name. You know how futile that is. You live in a cottage carved into a tree, so deep in the woods that no hiker or wanderer has ever passed by. You have no friends, and your relatives live not only far away but in residences at least as obscure as your own (consider Aunt Farfalee's tiny grotto, reachable only by swimming fifty feet underwater). You're not registered anywhere. You've never signed anything.

You return to the castle the next day, and the next. The king scowls murderously (what story *has* he been told?) as the queen runs through a gamut of guesses.

Althalos? Borin? Cassius? Cedric? Destrain? Fendrel? Hadrian? Gavin? Gregory? Lief? Merek? Rowan? Rulf? Sadon? Tybalt? Xalvador? Zane?

No no no no no no no no no no no no no no no and no. It's looking good.

But then, on the night of the second day, you make your fatal mistake. You'll wonder, afterward—why did I build a fire in front of the cottage tree, and do that little song and dance? It seemed harmless at the time, and you were so happy, so sure. You'd found yourself sitting alone in your parlor, thinking of where the cradle should go, wondering who'd teach you to fold a diaper, picturing the child's face as he looks up into yours and says, Father.

It's too much, just sitting inside like that, by yourself. It's too little. You hurry out into the blackness of the forest night, into the chirruping of the insects and the far-off hoots of the owls. You build a fire. You grant yourself a pint of ale, and then you grant yourself another.

And, almost against your own will, it seems that you're dancing around the fire. It seems that you've made up a song.

> *Tonight I brew, tomorrow I bake,*
> *And then the queen's child I will take.*
> *For little knows the royal dame . . .*

How likely is it that the youngest of the queen's messengers, the one most desperate for advancement, the one who's been threatened with dismissal (he's too avid and dramatic in his delivery of messages, he bows too low, he's getting on the king's nerves) . . . how likely is it that that particular young hustler, knowing every inch of the civilized kingdom to have been scoured already, every door knocked on, thought to go out into the woods that night, wondering if he was wasting precious time but hoping that maybe, maybe, the little man lived off the grid . . .

How likely is it that he sees your fire, creeps through the bracken, and listens to the ditty you're singing?

•

You return, triumphant, to the castle on the third and final afternoon. You are for the first time in your life a figure of power, of threat. Finally, you cannot be ignored or dismissed.

The queen appears to be flustered. She says, "Well, then, this is my last chance."

You have the courtesy to refrain from answering.

She says, "Is it Brom?"

No.

"Is it Leofrick?"

No.

"Is it Ulric?"

No.

Then there is a moment—a millimoment, the tiniest imaginable fraction of time—when the queen thinks of giving her baby to you. You see it on her face. There's a moment when she knows she could rescue you as you once rescued her; when she imagines throwing it all away and going off with you and her child. She does not, could not, love you, but she remembers standing in the room on that first night, when the straw started turning to gold; when she understood that an impossible situation had been met with an impossible result; when she thoughtlessly laid her hand on the sackcloth-covered gnarls of your shoulder . . . She thinks (*whoosh*, by the time you've read *whoosh*, she's no longer thinking of it) that she could leave her heartless husband, she could live in the woods with you and the child . . .

Whoosh.

The king shoots her an arctic glare. She looks at you, her

dark eyes avid and level, her neck arched and her shoulders flung back.

She speaks your name.

It's not possible.

The king grins a conquering, predatory grin. The queen turns away.

The world, which had been about to transform itself, changes back again. The world reveals itself to be nothing more than you, scuttling out of the throne room, hurrying through town, returning to the empty little house that's always there, that's always been there, waiting for you.

You stamp your right foot. You stamp it so hard, with such enchantment-compelled force, that it goes right through the marble floor, sinks to your ankle.

You stamp your left foot. Same thing. You are standing now, trembling, insane with fury and disappointment, ankle-deep in the royal floor.

The queen keeps her face averted. The king emits a peal of laughter that sounds like disdain itself.

And with that, you split in half.

It's the strangest imaginable sensation. It's as if some strip of invisible tape that's been holding you together, from mid-forehead to crotch, has suddenly been stripped away. It's no more painful than pulling off a bandage. And then you fall onto your knees, and you're looking at yourself, twice, both of you pitched forward, blinking in astonishment at a self who is blinking in astonishment at you, who are blinking in astonishment at him, who is blinking in astonishment at you . . .

The queen silently summons two of the guards, who lift you in two pieces from the floor in which you've become mired, who carry you, one half apiece, out of the room. They take you all the way back to your place in the woods, and leave you there.

There are two of you now. Neither is sufficient unto itself, but you learn, over time, to join your two halves together, and hobble around. There are limits to what you can do, though you're able to get from place to place. Each half, naturally enough, requires the cooperation of the other, and you find yourself getting snappish with yourself; you find yourself cursing yourself for your clumsiness, your overeagerness, your lack of consideration for your other half. You feel it doubly. Still, you go on. Still, you step in tandem, make your slow and careful way up and down the stairs, admonishing, warning, each of you urging the other to slow down, or speed up, or wait a second. What else can you do? Each would be helpless without the other. Each would be stranded, laid flat, abandoned, bereft.

STEADFAST; TIN

t's his lucky night. She's relented, after two years of aloof and chilly friendliness. Finally, cherries have appeared in all three of his slot machine windows. At the kegger thrown by his fraternity (it's spring by the calendar, but wind still knifes in off the lake, the grass is still sere), she's gotten a little drunker than she'd intended to, because she's just been abandoned by a boy she'd thought she might love; a boy who, when he left, took with him her first ideas about a cogent and convincing future.

At the frat party, her best friend whispers to her, *Go with that guy, give both of you a break, haven't you already observed your second anniversary of him mooning over you? And hey,* the friend whispers, *he's just hot enough and just dumb enough for tonight, which, honestly sweetheart, you could use right now, it's part of your recovery program, it's your post-asshole-boyfriend vacation, just take the poor fuck for a spin, it'll make you feel better, you need a little, how to put it, unintensity.*

He's drawn to remote girls, unavailable girls, girls who don't fall for it, being, as he is, a boy who might have been carved by Michelangelo; one of those exceptional beings who wear their beauty as if it were a common human state, and not an aberration. A remote and unavailable girl is rare for him.

Upstairs, in his room, he's got her shirt unbuttoned, he's fingering her crotch, which is pleasant for her, but only pleasant. She's been right, since he first locked eyes with her in Humanities 101—these hunky, uber-confident guys are never truly adept, they've never had to be, they've received their educations at the hands of girls who were too grateful, too enamored; girls who failed to teach them properly. This rough groping, these inexpert kisses, have been enough for those simple and besotted girls whose main objective was to keep him coming around. He must have had sex with a hundred girls, more than a hundred, and every one of them, it seems, has done little more than cooperate; than assure him that he's been right all along about what a girl wants, what a girl needs.

She's not that patient. She's not that interested.

So she steps back out of his embrace and strips, with the quick mechanical carelessness of a teammate in the locker room.

Oh. Well. Wow. This is a new one on him, this matter-of-fact, let's-get-on-with-it attitude.

It means he hasn't had time to prepare her, to slip her the abashed confession that's worked every other time, since he started college.

Disconcerted, confused, he strips as well. He can't think of anything else to do.

And there it is, unannounced.

All he can manage is "It's a prosthetic." He detaches it, tosses it carelessly, callously, onto the floor.

His right leg ends just above the knee.

Car accident, he tells her. When I was seventeen. The summer after high school.

The tossed-away lower leg sits on the floor. It looks like an accident, all by itself: the flesh-colored plastic calf tapering to an ankle that sprouts a toeless foot.

He stands before her. He has no trouble balancing on one leg.

He tells her—he always tells this story, to every girl—that the other car was driven by a fifteen-year-old who'd just stolen it, and was being chased by the police. It matters to him that he was not in any way at fault; that a young criminal, a demon of sorts, took his leg from him.

She needs a moment to fully apprehend the missing lower leg. His body, from the broad farmhand shoulders to the crop-rows of abdominals, is as flawless as she'd expected it to be.

He's harmed, though. He's been bluffing, since that car accident, which got him right after he'd emerged from high school, laureled and impeccable. It seems that some devil delivered the punch line before the joke had been set up, and that the joke, in its earliest stages (no time for a talking dog or a rabbi or a crazy wager), can deliver only a surreal and macabre finish.

So, this really handsome guy walks into a bar and . . . The bar blows up and kills everybody.

The bravado she's never liked in him, the thuggish self-assurance that's turned her off, reveals itself to have been a trick,

a way of coping. He's come off as cartoonishly confident because that's what he's needed to do.

He knows about damage the way a woman does. He knows,
the way a woman knows, how to carry on as if nothing's wrong.

Sometimes the fabric that separates us tears just enough for
love to shine through. Sometimes the tear is surprisingly small.

She marries not only a man but an inconsistency; she falls
in love with the gap between his physique and his affliction.

He marries the first girl who hasn't treated his amputation
as if it were no big deal; the first who doesn't need to evade his
sorrow and his anger or, worst of all, try talking him out of
his sorrow and his anger.

The surprises arrive in their own time.

After they're married, as year piles upon year, he's surprised by how often her abhorrence of sentimentality can render her cold and cruel; he's surprised by her insistence on calling
it "honesty." How is he supposed to fight with someone who
demands that her every lapse or failing be treated as a virtue,
as an admirable quality he refuses to understand?

She's surprised by how quickly his carelessly incandescent
beauty relaxes into the grinning, regular-guy appeal of a car
salesman; by the fact that he's become a car salesman; by the
ways in which his heftier, coarser flesh renders him less a sac-
rifice to some jealous god's wrath and more an everyday opti-
mist who's merely missing a leg.

He's surprised by how lonely he can feel in her presence, she by how she struggles to stay interested. Her foundering interest feeds his loneliness. His loneliness drives him to be more affable, more desperately charming, which further dulls her interest. It's not a good sign when she finds herself saying to him, over dinner in a restaurant, "For god's sake, will you stop acting like you're trying to sell me a *car*?" It's not a good sign when he has an affair with a foolish girl who listens raptly to his every opinion, laughs (perhaps a bit too riotously) at all his jokes.

The two stay married, though. They stay married because she took maternity leave when Trevor was born and, although she'd intended to, didn't go back to the law firm—she hadn't expected to be so endlessly fascinated by her infant son. They stay married because the remodeling of the kitchen is taking forever, because there's Beth now as well as Trevor, because the marriage isn't all that bad, because getting *un*married seems so difficult, so frightening, so sad. They can separate after the kitchen is finished; after the kids are a little older; after they as a couple have finally passed through the realm of irritation and bickering and reached the frozen waste of the unbearable.

They hope they'll learn to be happier together. They also yearn, sometimes, for the point at which misery becomes so profound as to leave them no alternative.

So, honey, did you like that story?
It was okay.
I've been saving that story. Until you were a little older.

Older?

Well, eight isn't old, it's just older than, you know, six. Why didn't you like it?

I hate it when you ask me that question. I said it was okay.

All right, let's phrase it a little differently. What didn't you like about it?

Can I go now?

In a minute. Would you answer the question, first?

You didn't read that story to Trevor. Trevor is outside, playing kickball.

I wanted to read this one specially to you. What didn't you like about it?

Okay. Why did that soldier have only one leg?

The toymaker ran out of lead.

It seemed kind of stupid. How the soldier fell in love with the ballerina because he thought she had one leg, too.

He could see only one of her legs. The other was raised up behind her.

But wouldn't he have known that? Hadn't he ever seen a ballerina before?

Maybe he hadn't. Or maybe it was wishful thinking. If you had just one leg, wouldn't you want to meet other people like you?

It doesn't make sense.

What doesn't?

The soldier falls out a window, some bad boys put him in a boat made of newspaper, and he sails down a storm drain.

That seems like it makes sense, to me.

But then he gets swallowed by a fish and the fish is bought by the same family's cook and when she cuts it open, the soldier's inside.

Why didn't you like that?

Uh, because it was stupid?

It was about destiny. Do you know what "destiny" means?

Yes.

The soldier and the ballerina couldn't be kept apart. That's destiny.

I know what it means. It's still stupid.

Maybe we could think of another word . . .

Then the little boy threw the soldier into the fireplace. For no reason. After the soldier came back, in the fish. The boy threw him into the fire.

A demon put a spell on the boy.

There's no such thing as demons.

Agreed. All right, let's say he didn't like it that the soldier was different.

You always say "different" when there's something wrong with somebody.

I'm not crazy about a phrase like "something wrong with somebody."

And then. You know what's really stupid? That the ballerina blows into the fireplace, too.

Could we talk about what "destiny" actually means?

The ballerina had both legs. The ballerina was up there on a shelf. The ballerina wasn't "different."

But she loved somebody who was.

What's the big deal, about being different? You make it sound like some kind of prize.

The marriage takes its turn on their twentieth anniversary, when the boat catches fire.

It occurs during the first vacation they've taken as a couple since the kids were born. Trevor is a freshman at Haverford, Beth is a junior in high school—they're pretty much grown up by now. And, according to the real estate agent, with the kitchen so meticulously redone, they could get a fortune for the house.

All their reasons are evaporating on them. They're taking the sort of save-the-marriage vacation that generally means the marriage is already lost.

The chartered sailboat, with its ten passengers and three-man crew, explodes in flames just off the Dalmatian Coast. They'll learn later about the drunken deckhand, the Zippo, the leak in a propane tank.

At one moment, they're sunning on the deck. She's noticed a cloud that looks like FDR's profile and is pointing it out to him, thinking this is what happy couples do; hoping that the impersonation of happiness will evolve into the genuine article. It helps, it seems to help, that they're spending two weeks in close quarters with eleven strangers; that they heard Eva Balderston say to her sister Carrie, "What a lovely couple," as they got up from dinner last night; that there are believers.

He's trying to make out FDR's profile in the cloud. She's

trying not to mind that he can't seem to see it, when it's so obviously *right there.* She's striving not to think about all he fails to notice in the world. He's fighting off his own burgeoning panic over letting her down again. He's about to say, "Oh, yeah, right, that's amazing," when in fact he sees only ordinary clouds . . .

The next moment, she's in the water. She knows there's been thunder, she knows there's been hot and blinding brilliance, but that reaches her as memory. She immediately inhabits a new impossibility, and for a moment it seems she's always been stroking through seawater, a mockingly tranquil, sparkling blue-green field on which, about thirty yards away, the boat's black silhouette is suspended in flames, like a skeleton on an orange X-ray screen.

A moment later, the actual starts reintroducing itself.

There's been an explosion. She seems to have been thrown clear. The pain in her left arm derives from a gash long and precise as the edge of a manila envelope. The idea of blood and sharks comes to her as a fact but only as a fact, a piece of long-remembered trivia, nothing actually threatening. It's as if she's recalling a story she heard about something awful that happened to a woman like her.

She seems to be surrounded by oddly random floating objects: a knob-ended length of mast, a baseball cap, an empty Diet Coke can.

She seems to see no one else.

As the ship begins its hissing descent into the water, it occurs to her that he's not much of a swimmer. He's refused the physical therapist's contention that swimming is the best exercise for an amputee.

She's surprised to find herself irritated with him. The irritation passes, and she's looking around again, as if awakened in an unfamiliar place, seeing no one but herself.

Her condition of stunned remove stays with her as she treads water, unsure about what else to do. It stays with her as the dark-haired man, who does not speak English, attaches the harness that pulls her upward. It does not abandon her until she finds herself strapped to a gurney in a helicopter, wearing a neck brace that permits only a view of two scuba tanks hanging from straps, and a white metal box emblazoned with a red cross.

The red cross means, somehow (it seems clear, if unfathomable), that her husband is dead. She's surprised (the baffled serenity of shock has not yet fully receded) by the piercing, inhuman wail she hears. She'd had no idea she could make a noise like that.

He will not be able to explain, because he will not remember, how he came to be lying in the shallows of a white-sand beach almost a full day after the boat caught fire. The medics who take him to the modest local hospital will merely say "Miracle," their accents rendering it "Me-wrack-cowl."

They bring her to him immediately. When she enters the hospital room he looks at her with chaste and monk-like calm, and then weeps as loudly and unabashedly as a three-year-old.

She gets into the narrow bed with him, and holds him. They both understand. They've visited a future in which for each of them the other has vanished. They've tasted separation. And now they've returned to the present, where a resurrection has occurred. They are, as of this hour, married forever.

Do you remember that story you read me?

What story? Hey, you're not packing your Britney Spears hoodie, are you?

I like my Britney hoodie. You know, that story.

I read you hundreds of stories. You haven't worn that hoodie since you were fifteen.

The story about the one-legged soldier.

Oh. Yes. Why are you bringing that up now?

Maybe because I'm leaving home.

You are not leaving home. You're going to college two states away. It's a six-hour drive. This will always be your home.

I'm not going to wear the Britney hoodie, what kind of dweeb do you think I am?

What is it about the one-legged soldier?

I knew what you were doing. I thought I should tell you I knew what you were doing. Now that I'm leaving home.

And what, darling, do you think I was doing?

Duh. You were telling me the story of you and Dad.

If you're not going to wear the hoodie, why are you taking it at all?

Sentimental reasons. A reminder of my glory days.

Your glory days are still ahead of you.

People keep saying that. What point were you trying to make, reading me that story?

I don't think I was trying to make a point at all. It was just a story.

It was just the only story there is about somebody who's missing a leg, and gets followed into a fire by his ballerina girlfriend.

Do you really think I was trying to make some kind of point about your father and me?

I remember you asking me if I knew what the word "destiny" meant.

I guess I wondered . . . If you were worried. About your father and me.

Fucking right I was.

I'm not crazy about that word.

Tell me you never noticed that Trevor and I knew how miserable you both were. You seem to be getting better, though.

Leave the hoodie here, all right?

I'm perfectly capable of keeping it safe, all on my own, in my dorm room. This hoodie does not need to reside within the House of Safety.

Honestly? I'm not really sure what we're talking about, anymore.

We're talking about a paper ballerina who had two perfectly good legs of her own but flew into the fire anyway.

It's silly for you to pack something you're never going to wear. Dorm rooms have extremely limited storage space.

Okay, let's keep the hoodie here. Let's keep everything here.

Please don't be melodramatic.

Trevor's gone. I leave tomorrow.

And you keep saying that because . . .

That story was all about the paper ballerina. She didn't have a destiny. Only the one-legged soldier did.

Do you want us to read the story again?

I think I'd rather eat glass.

All right, then.

I'm going to leave the hoodie here. It'll be safer here.

Good. It's nice to be told I'm right about something. Some little thing. Every now and then.

They're into their sixties now.

He's still selling cars. She's returned to her practice, knowing she's too old and yet too inexperienced to rise above the level of associate. The firm is doing well enough to have room for a competent-enough tough-but-compassionate mother figure. She's not only there to litigate, but to be salty and irreverent for men whose own mothers tended to be prim, mannerly, and cheerful almost to the point of madness.

She minds, more than she'd thought she would, that she appears to others as a cantankerous, endearing old lady.

He's worried about sales. Nobody wants American cars anymore.

The two of them are at home tonight, as they are most nights.

He's become the only person to whom she remains visible, who knows that she hasn't always been old. Beth and Trevor love her but so clearly want her to be, to always have been, grandmotherly: reliable and harmless and endlessly patient.

The next surprise to come, it seems, is true decline. The surprise after that is mortality, first one of them, then the other.

Her therapist encourages her not to think this way. She does her best.

Here they are, in their living room. They've built a fire in the fireplace. The movie they've been watching on their big-screen TV has just ended. His prosthetic (it's titanium, beautiful in its way, nothing like the grotesque, Band-Aid-colored appendage of their college days) stands beside the fireplace. As the closing credits roll, they sit together, companionably, on the sofa.

She says, "Call me old-fashioned, but I still like a movie with a happy ending."

Watching the credits roll, he wonders: Have we reached our happy ending?

It feels happy enough, in its modest, domestic way. And there've been happy endings already.

There was that night in his fraternity-house room, forty years ago, when he took off his clothes and revealed the damage that had been done to him; when she did not, like so many girls before her, insist that it was no big deal. There's the fact that they didn't have sex until the following night, and when they did have sex on the following night he was already halfway in love with her, because she was able to look at him and apprehend his loss.

That was a happy ending.

There was the sight of her walking into that hospital room, and his sudden, surprising awareness that he wanted to see nobody more urgently than he wanted to see her. That only she could get him out of there and take him home.

There was the night Trevor came out to him, at Beth's engagement party, when they found themselves alone together with brandy and cigars; the night he realized that Trevor had decided to tell his father first (aren't the sister or mother usually the first to be told?); the chance Trevor gave him to hold his trembling and frightened son, to assure him that it didn't make any difference, to feel his son's worried head burrowed gratefully into his chest.

That was another happy ending.

He could name dozens of others. A camping trip when, as the first light struck Half Dome, he knew that Beth, age four, was comprehending the terrible clarity of beauty, for the first time. A sudden rainstorm that soaked the whole family so thoroughly that they danced in it, kicking up puddles.

There's this text from Beth, sent less than an hour ago, a selfie of her and her husband, Dan, in their kitchen on an ordinary night (the baby must have been asleep by then), their heads pressed together, smiling into Beth's iPhone, with only the message, XXX.

Beth wasn't required to send that text, not on a random and unremarkable night. She wasn't meeting expectations. She'd simply wanted to show herself, herself and her husband, to her mother and father, so they'd know where she was, and who she was with. It seems that that matters to her, their younger child, the thornier and more argument-prone one. It seems that she's twenty-four, happily married (please, Beth, stay happy even if you don't stay married); it seems that she wants to locate herself to, and for, her parents. It seems that she knows (she'd know) how future nights lie waiting; how there's no way of determining their nature but it's probably not a bad idea to transmit a fragment of this night, when she's young, and thrilled by her life, when she and Dan (stubbled, bespectacled, smitten by his wife, maybe dangerously so) have put the baby down and are making dinner together in their too-small apartment in New Haven.

Happy endings. Too many to count.

There's the two of them on the sofa, with a fire in the fireplace; there's his wife saying, "Time for bed," and him agreeing that it is in fact time for bed, in a few minutes, after the fire has burned itself out.

She gets up to stir the last of the embers. As she scatters the embers she sees, she could swear she sees . . . *something* in the dying flames, something small and animate, a tiny sphere of what she can think of only as livingness. A moment later, it resolves itself into mere fire.

She doesn't ask him if he's seen it, too. But by now she and he are sufficiently telepathic that he knows to say, "Yes," without the slightest idea of what he's agreeing to.

BEASTS

ou've met the beast. He's ahead of you at the convenience store, buying smokes and a Slim Jim, flirting with the unamused Jamaican cashier. He's slouching across the aisle on the Brooklyn-bound G train, sinewy forearms crawling with tattoos. He's holding court—crass and coke-fueled, insultingly funny—at the after-hours party your girlfriend has insisted on, to which you've gone because you're not ready, not yet, to be the kind of girl who wouldn't.

You may find yourself offering yourself to him.

Because you're sick of the boys who want to get to know you before they'll sleep with you ("sleep with you" is the phrase they use); the boys who ask, apologetically, if they came too soon; who call the next day to tell you they had a really great time.

Or because you're starting to worry that a certain train is about to leave the station; that although you'll willingly board a different train, one bound for marriage and motherhood, that train may take its passengers to a verdant and orderly realm from which few ever return; that the few who try to return discover that what's felt like mere hours to them has been twenty years back home; that they feel grotesque and desperate at parties they could swear had wanted them, had pawed and nuzzled them, just last night, or the night before.

Or because you believe, you actually believe, you can undo the damage others have done to the jittery, gauntly handsome guy with the cigarettes and the Slim Jim, to the dour young subway boy, to the glib and cynical fast-talker who looks at others as if to say, *Are you an asshole or a fool?*, those being his only two categories.

Beauty was the eldest of three sisters. When the girls' father went off to the city on business, and asked his daughters what presents they'd like him to bring back, the two younger girls asked for finery. They asked for silk stockings, for petticoats, for laces and ribbons.

Beauty, however, asked only for a single rose, a rose like any that could have been snipped from a half dozen or more bushes not fifty feet from the family's cottage.

Her point: Bring back from your journey something I could easily procure right here. My desire for treasure is cleansed of greed by the fact that I could fulfill it myself, in minutes, with a pair of garden shears. I'm moved by the effort, not the object; a demand for something rare and precious can only turn devotion into errand.

Was she saying as well, *Do you really imagine a frock or hair ribbon will help? Do you think it'll improve the ten or so barely passable village men, or alter the modest hope that I will, at least, not end up marrying Claude the hog butcher, or Henri with the withered arm? Do you believe a petticoat could be compensation for our paucity of chances?*

I'd rather just have a rose.

The father did not comprehend any of that. He was merely surprised, and disappointed, by the modesty of Beauty's request. He'd been saving up for this trip; he'd finally found a potential buyer for his revolutionary milking machine; he was at long last a man with a meeting to go to; he liked the idea of returning from a business trip as treasure-laden as a raja.

That's all you want, Beauty?

That's all.

You're sure? You're not going to be disappointed when Cheri and Madeline are trying on their new frocks?

No. I'll love my rose.

There was no point in telling him that Cheri and Madeline were inane; that the finery he'd bring them was destined to be worn once or twice, at village parties, and then folded into a drawer, to be looked at wistfully every now and then after their husbands and children kept them housebound; after the silks and crinolines were so peppered with moth holes they were no longer wearable anyway.

A single rose it would be, then, for Beauty. She who possessed a sharper and less sentimental mind than her sisters. She who knew there was no point in acquiring anything she didn't have already, because there was no future she couldn't read in the dung-strewn streets of the village, in the lewd grins of the young chimney sweep, or the anticipatory silence of the miller's boy.

All right, then. A rose was what she wanted. A rose was what she would get.

The father, on his way back from his trip to the city (the meeting with the buyer had not gone well), stopped on the verge of a castle surrounded by lush gardens. He needed, after all, to pick a rose that grew close to the village, or else he'd have nothing for Beauty but a stem and a few withered leaves when he got home.

Grumbling, annoyed by his daughter's perverse and hostile modesty (but relieved as well that, unlike her sisters, she wasn't costing him money he'd recently learned he would not receive), he plucked a rose from a particularly abundant bush. One rose out of thousands.

Wrong castle. Wrong rosebush.

The beast pounced on the father. The beast was more than eight feet tall, a hybrid of wolf and lion, with bright, murderous eyes and thickly furred arms bigger than the father's waist. The beast was somehow all the more menacing for the fact that he wore a waistcoat over a ruffled shirt.

He proclaimed rose-stealing a capital crime. He raised a paw like a bouquet of daggers. He was about to peel the father's face from his skull, and work his way down from there.

Please, sir, the rose was for my daughter!

Stealing is stealing.

Imagine a voice like a lawn mower on gravel. Try not to think about the beast's breath.

She's the loveliest and most innocent girl in the world. I offered to buy her anything she wanted, and all she asked for was a rose.

The beast paused over that.

She could have had anything, and she asked for a rose?

She's an unusual girl. I love her as I love life itself.

The beast lowered his paw, thrust it forcefully into the pocket of his coat, as if to keep it from striking out on its own.

Go home, then. Say goodbye to your daughter. Give her the rose. Then come back here and accept your punishment.

I will.

If you're not back by this time tomorrow, I'll hunt you down and kill your daughters before I kill you.

The beast turned and strode back to his castle, on legs big and powerful as a bison's. The father, clutching the rose, leapt onto his horse and rode away.

When the father reached home he told his daughters the story, said he'd be off on the morrow, at dawn, to be flayed by the beast.

His younger daughters assured him it was all bluff. The beast couldn't possibly know where they lived. The beast was a standard-issue psychopath. Threats are easy to deliver; the beast was surely on to other hallucinations already. The beast was probably, at that very moment, trying to figure out who

was whispering obscenities from the cupboards, or why the fur-
niture kept rearranging itself.

So, Poppa, could we see what you brought us?

Oh, yes, of course . . .

He began removing the parcels from his saddlebag.

Only Beauty knew that the beast would track them down,
and murder them. Only Beauty understood what a single rose
might signify, what acts a rose could inspire, if you lived without hope. If you were a beast confined to a castle, or a girl confined to an obscure and unprosperous village.

And so, after midnight, when her father and sisters were
asleep, Beauty slipped out to the stable, mounted her father's
horse, and told it to take her to the beast's castle. The horse,
being a beast itself, was more than ready to comply.

It looked like an act of ultimate self-sacrifice. That was not
untrue. But it was also true that Beauty preferred whatever the
beast might do to another day of tending the geese, another
night of needlepoint.

It was true as well that she hoped her father might come
for her, when he woke at daybreak and saw she was gone. It
was true that she entertained images of her father confronting
the beast—her father who'd been the beast of her youth, enormous and bristling with hair; her father who'd been ostenta-
tiously kind and gentle even as she, unblinded by the naïveté
her sisters enjoyed, understood the effort required of him to
refrain from certain acts he could so easily have committed,

with the girls' mother safely absent under her cross in the churchyard.

Beauty speculated, as the horse took her through nocturnal field and chirruping fen to the beast's castle, over the battle she might be inspiring. She took (why deny it?) a certain pleasure in wondering who would claim her—father or fiend?

The father was, in fact, stricken when morning broke and he found that his eldest daughter had gone to the beast. Still, he couldn't help thinking that her desire for the rose had not only caused this trouble but was, in its way, an insidious form of vanity. Beauty wanted, didn't she, to be the pure and faultless one. She was subject to the arrogance of nuns.

He would be harmed forever by his decision to let her take his place. But that's what he did. He would, over time, discover more and various ways to blame his daughter. He'd sink with a certain sensuousness into the image of himself as an awful man, a heartless man, which would prove, over time, an easier man for him to be.

From the moment Beauty arrived at the beast's palace, she was impeccably treated. Meals served themselves, fireplaces ignited merrily when she entered rooms. Childlike arms, manifestations of the plaster walls, offered lit candelabra to guide her through the crepuscular hallways.

She needed less than two days to understand that her father

would not mount a rescue; that he was grateful for his own deliverance; that an unthreatened dotage with two out of three daughters (the two could be relied upon to fuss over his aching joints, to wonder if he needed another pillow) struck him as sufficient.

Beauty lived alone, then, with the beast in his castle.

He was always courtly and gentle. No vulpine sex was visited upon the innocent girl in the enormous bed, in which she slept alone. She did not find herself impaled on a lurid red member just under two feet long; she was not tongued in a manner more carnivorous than carnal; she was not subject to a lust that had nothing to do with her own pleasure.

She was, of course, relieved. She could barely admit to herself that she was also, in some dark and secret way, disillusioned.

The days and nights took on a strange but palpable regularity. By day the beast pretended to duties in remote parts of the castle. By night, after he'd sat with Beauty as she ate her dinner, he stalked the halls, muttering, until it was time for him to stumble out into the forest, tear the throat from a fawn or boar, and devour it.

Beauty knew about that only because she happened to look out her bedroom window, late one sleepless night. The beast believed he killed his animals in secret. He didn't understand Beauty's capacity to accept the fact that, like everybody, he was tormented, but also, like everybody, he needed to eat.

He was, and was not, what she'd expected. She'd known,

of course, that he'd be wild and dangerous and smelly. She had not anticipated this creaturely but chivalrous routine.

If Beauty was surprisingly let down by the beast's immaculate behavior, by his secrecy regarding his less presentable habits, she did develop, over time, a mild but persistent affection for him. Not for the zoo stench—scat mingled with rage—that no cologne could cover; not for the sight of claws bigger than roofing nails, struggling to pick up a wine goblet. She grew fond of his determination to act kindly and tenderly, to be generous and true, as if she were a wife long married to a man whose carnal wishes had abandoned him, along with his youthful self-regard, but who feared more than anything the loss of his wife's affection as she lived on with his milder self. She came to harbor feelings inspired by the gentleness the beast forced himself to summon, the gratitude apparent in his inhuman eyes when he gazed at her, the condition of brave hopelessness that was his life.

Finally, after months had passed, with their succession of identical days and nights—Beauty's distracted engagement in idle embroidery, dinners at which there was nothing to say— the beast told her to go home again. He sank massively to his knees before her, like an elk shot full of arrows, and said he'd been wrong to keep her with him, he'd been subject to some fantasy about love's power, but really, what had he been thinking? Had he actually believed that a pretty girl, come to him against her will, could love a monster? He'd been duped, it seemed, by stories he'd heard about girls who loved misshapen and appalling creatures. He had not thought to wonder what might be wrong, in such cases, with the girls themselves.

Beauty could not find a way to tell him that, had he been less mannerly, had he offered her a more potent aspect of threat, it might have worked. She wondered to herself why so many men seemed to think meekness was what won women's hearts.

But she and the beast had developed no habits of candor, and it was too late, by then, to start. She accepted the beast's offer, and fled. She was sorry about forsaking him, but could not bring herself to embrace such a maidenly future, bored, unchallenged, sequestered in a castle—however accommodating it might be, however prone to the lighting of fires and the laying out of meals—that offered by way of companionship only a monster obsessed with contemplating his own sins. She fled because life in the beast's castle was more comfortable but not, in its deepest heart, substantially different from the life she'd lived at home.

When she returned to her village, however, she was surprised to find that she experienced no sense of going home. She was happy, happy enough, to see her father and sisters again, but her father was still the man who hadn't followed her to the beast's castle and done battle for her. Her sisters had married the men they were destined to marry—a brick mason and an ironmonger, sturdily prosaic men who performed their jobs with neither complaint nor ardor, who liked their dinners served promptly at six, and who stumbled home late from the pubs to set about begetting still more children. Beauty's middle sister had two babies already; the youngest was suckling her first, with a second on the way.

What was most surprising, though, was the fact that Beauty seemed to have developed a reputation while she'd been away.

Although the true story of her time with the beast did not get around, no one believed her father's version, about her sudden departure for a convent. The villagers agreed that she'd been misbehaving in a remote and foreign place, and that, once some duke or earl had tired of her, or she'd grown too familiar to be the pick of the bawdy house, she was deluded enough to think she could simply come back, as if nothing had happened. Now that Beauty was home again, even the pick of the still-unmarried men (the baker prone to unpredictable spasms of rage, the rabbit-keeper with the squint and the tic)—even those sad specimens—were reluctant about a girl with a past that clearly required a cover-up.

Eventually, late one night (explanations would have been awkward), Beauty slipped away, mounted the horse, and rode back to the beast's castle. At least she was wanted there. At least she was loved. At least the beast saw no reason for her to be ashamed.

The castle, however, when she arrived, was dark and empty. Its massive doors swung open easily enough, but the candlesticks on the walls did not light themselves as she moved down the hallways. The cherub faces in the molding were merely carved, unliving wood.

She found the beast in the garden, which had turned weedy and rank, its hedges throwing out branches like panicky, irrational thoughts. The fountain, gone dry, was etched all over with hairline cracks.

There, on the paving stones before the arid fountain, lay the beast.

Beauty knelt beside him. Although he was too far gone to speak, she could still see a flicker in his yellow eyes.

She lifted, with effort, one of his paws in her small hands. She told him quietly, as if it were a secret, that she'd realized she loved him only by being parted from him. She wasn't lying; she wasn't exactly lying. She did love him, in a way. She pitied him, she pitied herself, she grieved for both of them—souls who seemed to have gotten so easily and accidentally lost.

And if he could be healed, if he might be brought back from death's brink . . .

She loved the image of herself turning proudly from the low lot of village men who'd deign to have her; she loved the idea of saying no to the baker and the rabbit-keeper and the filmy-eyed old widower whose once-respectable house was going slant on its foundation, shedding shingles into the town square.

She would be the bride of a beast. She would live in his castle. She would care nothing for the whispers of biddies and gossips.

She said softly, into the beast's furry ear, which was bigger than a catcher's mitt, that if he could revive himself, if he could manage to rise again, she'd marry him.

The results were instantaneous.

The beast leapt up with a lion's fervor. Behind him, the fountain spurted water again.

Beauty stepped back. The beast looked adoringly at her. He looked at her with a thankfulness that was marvelous and, somehow, dreadful to see.

In less than a moment, the beast's hide split open like a chrysalis. The claws and fangs fell away. The feral reek evaporated.

And here he is.

He's stunning. He's sturdy, square-faced, snapping with muscle.

The prince stands among the snarls of shed fur, the claws that litter the paving stones. He looks down in amazement at his restored body. He flexes his human hands, tests the athletic springiness of legs that are no longer taloned haunches.

The spell has been broken. Did Beauty suspect it, all along? She'll enjoy the idea that she'd intuited it, that she was a girl who could ferret out the workings of enchantment, but she'll never be sure.

She waits breathlessly, ecstatically, for the newly summoned prince to take her in his arms. But first he has to check his reflection in the water, which is already rippling in the revived fountain.

It's worked. He's managed it. He's seduced a lovely woman into pledging her troth to a soul that's been concealed—to everyone but her—by disfigurement.

Beauty's pale bosom heaves with anticipation.

The prince turns slowly from his own reflection, shows

her a lascivious, bestial smile; a rapacious and devouring smile. Although his face is impeccably handsome, something about it is not quite right. The eyes remain feral. The mouth seems capable, still, of tearing out the throat of a deer. He could almost be the beast's younger, handsomer (much handsomer) brother, as if his parents had produced a deformed child and then a beautiful, perfectly proportioned one.

Beauty begins, suddenly, to wonder. Is it possible that the beast-spell was meant, long ago, as protection? Had the prince been locked into a monster's guise for decipherable reasons?

She backs away. Grinning victoriously, emitting a low growl of triumph, he advances.

HER HAIR

fter the witch caught on . . .

after she cut off Rapunzel's hair . . .

after the prince fell from the tower onto the thornbush, which pricked out his eyes . . .

He wandered the world searching for her, astride his horse. He took no one with him other than the horse.

He knocked on a thousand doors. He rode along village streets and down country lanes, calling out her name. Her name was sufficiently strange that the villagers and farmers he passed assumed him to be deranged. It never occurred to them that he might be seeking an actual person.

Some were helpful: *There's a river ahead, watch out for the gully coming up.* Some threw stones at him, some flicked switches at his horse's gaunt flanks.

He didn't stop. He searched for a year.

Until, finally, he found her . . .

he found her in the desert shanty to which the witch had banished her . . .

he found her living alone, with dust devils swirling through the curtains, with flies thicker than the dust . . .

She knew him the moment she opened the door, though he was all but unrecognizable by then, sallow and torn, his raiment in rags.

And there were those empty black sockets, the size of ravens' eggs, where his eyes had been.

He said only, "Rapunzel." A word he'd spoken at a thousand thresholds already, and been a thousand times turned away, either cruelly or kindly, for the destitute and deranged creature he'd become. There is, as he'd learned, a surprisingly fine line between a prince on a quest and an addled, eyeless wanderer who has nothing more useful to offer than that single, incomprehensible word.

He'd come to know the condition of the benighted; he who had, a year earlier, been regal and splendid, broad and brave, climbing hand over hand up a rope of golden hair.

When he stood finally at her doorway, having sensed the presence of a house, having felt his way along its splintery boards until he touched a threshold . . .

when she reached out to touch his scabbed and bleeding hand, he recognized her fingers a moment before they made contact with his skin, the way a dog knows its master is approaching, while still a block away. He emitted a feral moan, which might have been ecstasy or might have been intolerable pain, as if there existed a sound that could convey both at the same time.

He couldn't cry. He had no more apparatus for that.

Before he and Rapunzel left for his castle, she made a quick excuse, ran back into the shanty, and took her hair out of the bureau drawer in which she'd been keeping it all the past year, wrapped in tissue, as safe and sequestered as the family silver.

She hadn't looked at it, not once, since the witch took her to the shanty.

What if it had turned drab and lusterless . . .

what if it was infested with mites . . .

what if it simply looked . . . dead . . . like an artifact in some small local museum . . .

But there it was, two twenty-foot-long red-blond skeins, intertwined, shining, healthy as a well-fed cat.

She slipped the hair into her bag before leaving with the prince.

They live in the castle now. Every night the prince lies beside her and caresses her hair, which she keeps by the bedside . . .

which she washes and perfumes . . .

which she pulls out discreetly, as the prince finds his way into bed.

He buries his face in her hair. Sometimes she wonders— why doesn't he ask how the hair still grows from her head? Didn't he see it severed by the witch? He can't possibly imagine it's grown back in only a year.

But he still, with his eyeless face swaddled by her hair, lets out (though less and less often) that terrible howl, that protestation of revelation and loss, that mewling tentative as a kitten's yet loud as a leopard's growl.

It seems he's either forgotten or prefers not to remember. So she never reminds him that the hair is no longer attached . . .

she never reminds him it's not a living thing any longer . . .

she never reminds him it's a memory that she keeps intact, that she maintains in the present, for him.

Why would he want to know?

EVER/AFTER

nce, in time, a prince lived in a castle on a knoll, under a sky brightened by the royal blue of the harbor. Arrayed along the slope that descended from castle to harbor was a town in which carpenters made widely coveted tables and chairs, and bakers baked cakes and pies that people traveled some distance to procure. Every morning, the local fishermen hauled in nets full of sparkling silver fish; every night the smell of grilling fish filled the air. The avenue that skirted the harbor was lit by cafés and taverns, from which music and laughter were gently wind-borne throughout the town and into the forest, where hares and pheasants paused occasionally to listen.

When the prince turned eighteen, he was married to a princess from a nearby, less prosperous kingdom; an inland kingdom built on a river centuries dry; a place where the chalky soil produced only cabbages and parsnips and other such hearty but uncompelling vegetables; where the cafés were all closed by nine o'clock and the local artisans produced nothing but coarse, heavy woolen blankets and jerseys, which were offered optimistically as the best defense against the icy winds that blew from the glacier on the mountaintop.

The princess's hand was sought for the prince by the prince's father, the king, as protection against the day when the princess's kingdom sent its soldiers—scrawny and weak from their meager diet, but all the more dangerous for their endless feelings of deprivation—bearing bows and longswords, into the verdancy and abundance of the kingdom on the harbor, and declared it rightfully theirs.

The princess's father agreed, in part because he had too little confidence in his own starved and sullen army, and in part because the princess in question, the eldest of his three daughters, the one most lacking in traditional charms, had received no other offers by the age of twenty-two, but was required by law to be married before marriage could be permitted either of her younger sisters, both of whom (it struck the king as a cruel joke) were lithe and lovely.

The marriage did not go well, at first. The prince recognized his duty, and performed it. The princess did, as well. The princess, being other than beautiful, needed no delusions about how a deal had been struck, how she had been foisted off on a husband who would, she believed, carry out the perfunctory marital duties and then set about on his true amorous vocation with chambermaids and duchesses and the occasional harlot, smuggled in from town.

She was, as it turned out, mistaken.

Although, during the wedding (which was also the occasion of their first meeting) and immediately after, he struck her as posturing and false—a prince who seemed to have been inexpertly instructed in the ways of princes (*Hold your head a little higher, no, not quite that high; speak in a commanding tone . . . No, that doesn't mean shout . . .*)—he soon proved not to be, as she'd expected, deceitfully confident about the skills he lacked. He was handsome, far handsomer than she, but his beauty was milky and ephemeral, moist-eyed; he was one of those delicate boys of whom, by the time he'd turned fifty, others would whisper, "You wouldn't believe it, he was once such a pretty boy," in tones of scandalized satisfaction.

But, more unexpected . . . he was so nervous, so unsure, that he could not imagine himself as king, though his becoming king one day was inevitable as mortality itself. All of which he confessed to her, immediately, on their wedding night. It did not seem to occur to him that a fear might go unspoken, that anxiety could be masked.

He, for his part, was initially disappointed, but soon surprised by her, as well.

When she first appeared to him, on their wedding day, her bridal finery, however artful, could not disguise her heftiness, the great dome of her forehead or the stunted apostrophe of her nose. She might have been a barge, steered by her father with the steady determination of commerce along the cathedral aisle. This, then, would be the face, these would be the mannish shoulders and the breadth of hip, he'd be seeing, daily, for the rest of his life.

And yet, on their wedding night, when they were finally alone together in the royal bedchamber . . . Let's say she could not have been the virgin that tradition and propriety demanded her to be. She couldn't have invented tricks like that, untutored. Who knew how many stableboys, how many pages, she had pushed down onto haystack or secluded lawn?

He liked not only the fleshly revelations—he who was, in fact, as virginal as she was supposed to be—but the evidence that she had been ill-behaved. He liked as well his first sight of her nakedness. She was stocky but firm, her body all hillocks and white, satiny risings. On that first night she told him, unembarrassed, what to do, and he, being inexperienced, was glad to obey; he who faced a future of issuing commands, of others looking at him questioningly, waiting for him to make the decision, every decision, every time.

The king died soon after, trampled on a hunt by the very horse he'd considered his truest companion. The prince was, to his horror, made king three weeks before his nineteenth birthday.

She fell into love with a strange sense of powerlessness, as if she and her husband had contracted the same disease at the same time. She looked forward to the mornings, seeing him groggy but sweet upon awakening (he liked to be held, just for a few minutes, before getting out of bed and attending to his kingly duties); she liked talking to him at night, after the duties had been dispatched, about everything, from the small particulars of the day to his love of a local poet, recently deceased, from whose work the new king could quote, at length. She was surprised (and oddly, if only briefly, disappointed) to find that she'd been wrong about the chambermaids and harlots; that he actually intended, every night, to return to their bed; that he did not cease to delight in her willingness to command (*Hold still, relax, I know it hurts a little but give in to it, pain in moderation has its pleasures . . .*)

During the months after his coronation, it was increasingly impossible for her to believe that he undervalued her intelligence (she was, in fact, intelligent). It was ever more apparent that he prized her opinions over those of his counselors (she whose only official purposes were peacekeeping and the production of heirs). By the time he'd turned twenty (just after she'd turned twenty-four), it was evident that they ruled together, secretly; that he (as tradition demanded) would offer as his own pronouncements, every day, that which they had decided together, the night before, when they were alone, in bed.

Decades passed. They had a son, a daughter, and a second son.

Their lives, their reign, was not untroubled. Among their subjects there were robberies, contract disputes, lawsuits over property lines that had been drawn a century ago. The axemaker's wife beat her husband to death with a lamb bone and, as the police took her away, proclaimed that she hadn't wanted to sully one of the axes. In the castle, a maid was impregnated by a page, and (although the king and queen would not have punished her) drowned herself in a well. The cook fought continually with the housekeeper, each delivering, for almost thirty years, a weekly report about the excesses and callousness of the other.

Among the family, the daughter, the middle child, who had not only inherited but doubled her mother's tendency to corpulence, jumped out a window at the age of twelve, but—it being only a second-story window—landed unharmed on a hydrangea bush and, having made the gesture once, seemed to feel no need of making it again.

The second son, the youngest child—knowing he'd never be king—ran off when he turned seventeen, but returned less than a year later, thin and ragged, having tried to live as a bard and troubadour in a neighboring kingdom, but having found that his limited gifts attracted scant attention. He decided he could manage as a prince, composing verses and singing songs at occasional palace recitals.

The oldest boy was almost suspiciously untroubled. He was hale and stalwart, confident without an edge of arrogance, but his was not the most subtle and penetrating of minds, and it was impossible for his parents to refrain from periods of doubt about his ability to be king himself when the day arrived.

Although the king and queen never ceased entirely to worry over their children, the older boy remained true and devoted, and took on a more royal aspect as he entered his twenties. The younger boy married a homely but insightful princess from several kingdoms away, wrote volumes of verse for his wife, who believed him to be a genius, unheralded in his time but sure to be vindicated by history. The daughter did not marry (though she had offers) but became an expert archer, a hunter, and a sailor, and took great joy in everything she did so well.

The king and queen themselves were not untouched by sorrows or trials. In late middle age, the king believed himself to have fallen in love with an absurd but imperiously serene, lunar and ethereally pallid duchess, and needed a fortnight to learn that she intoxicated but bored him. The queen, soon after the duchess episode, returned to her old habit of pushing pages and stableboys down onto hay bales and secluded lawns, until the boys' helpless willingness, the thoughts of advancement that were audible through their lascivious moans, became more humiliating than gratifying.

The king and queen returned to each other, battered, humbled, and strangely amused by their escapades. They found, to their mutual surprise, that they seemed to love each other more rather than less for having shown, rather late in the game, this capacity for their blood to rise.

She said to him, on occasion, *I'm turning slender and sly, I'm learning to weep discreetly when the nightingale sings.*

He said to her, on occasion, *Straddling me won't raise you any higher, are you sure it's worth the effort?*

Which (to their shared surprise) always made them both laugh.

Eventually, decades later, when the king was dying, the queen gently ushered everybody out into the corridor, closed the door to the royal bedchamber, and got into bed with her husband.

She started singing to him. They laughed. He was short of breath, but he could still laugh. They asked each other, Is this silly? Is this . . . pretentious? But they both knew that everything there was to say had been said already, over and over, across the years. And so the king, relieved, released, free to be silly, asked her to sing him a song from his childhood. He didn't need to be regal anymore, he didn't need to seem commanding or dignified, not with her. They were, in their way, dying together, and they both knew it. It wasn't happening only to him. So she started singing. They shared one last laugh—they agreed that the cat had a better voice than she did. Still, she sang him out of the world.

When the queen was dying, years later, there were twenty-three people in the room, as well as three cats and two dogs. There were her children and their children and their children's children, three of her maids, two pages (the older and the younger, long known to be lovers, their secret honored by everyone), and the cook and the housekeeper (who'd delivered their final complaints only weeks earlier). The animals—the dogs and cats—were in bed with the queen. The people knew, somehow, to stand at a certain distance, except for Sophia, the oldest maid, who moistened the queen's brow with a handkerchief.

The room wasn't silent, or reverent. One of the babies fussed. One of the dogs snarled at one of the cats. But the queen, who was enormous by then, and pale as milk, looked at all the beings surrounding her, human and animal, with a certain grave compassion, as if they were the ones who were dying.

Just before she passed away, a grandchild said to another, "She's like a planet, don't you think?"

The other replied, "No, she's like a sick old lady."

Each felt pleased by the proof of the other's foolishness. Each boy, as their grandmother the queen sank away, thought of his own promising future; one because he had a poet's eye and heart; the other because he was unsentimental and true. Each believed, as their grandmother died, that he'd go far in the world.

As it turned out, both of them were right.

All the children prospered, after the queen had been put to rest. Her eldest son, who had, at his mother's insistence, ruled since his father's death, remained just and benevolent, and the male heir produced so quickly by his wife looked, early on, to be another compassionate king-in-the-making. The castle did not crack or crumble. Every tide brought in new swarms of fish. The sons and daughters of the carpenters made tables and chairs even more marvelous than those their parents had produced; the sons and daughters of the bakers rose early every morning to produce more pies and cakes, more bread and muffins.

There was, in general, peace, though robberies and contract disputes continued; sons and daughters still occasionally ran off, or lost their minds; irritation, long harbored, still festered occasionally into murder.

Nevertheless, overall, there was abundance and grace. There

were marriages that lasted lifetimes. There were festivals and funerals, there were artisans and poets. Inventors produced mechanisms that shed clearer light, that uncomplainingly performed the drearier tasks, that captured and held music long thought to exist only as long as the players played and the singers sang. In the forest, the hares and pheasants paused occasionally, with the same surprised interest, at the sound of music, and did not know or care whether the music emanated from living musicians or from musicians long dead. In town, children—all of whom had been born long after the old king and queen were laid side by side in their sarcophagi—discerned, from among the music and the laughter that emanated from cafés, their parents, calling them home. Some went willingly, some went grudgingly, but all of them, every child, returned home, every night.